P9-BBP-401

The day was dark as night . . .

Then a hard, white glare of lightning almost blinded me. The cracking boom of thunder seemed to shake the ground under my feet. The cottonwood trees thrashed their branches overhead.

I made a great target for lightning bolts as I ran across the empty expanse of lawn. Suddenly a feeling of absolute doom gripped me and stopped me in my tracks. I looked up, my eyes irresistibly drawn to the porch at the second story. Thick clouds roiled above Cottonwood Hall, but for a moment the wind dropped, as if in a sudden vacuum.

I saw a face, a white face on the porch. The body that had to be there to go with the face was invisible, lost in the surrounding darkness.

The face stared at me. From that height I could not possibly see its expression, but from its burning eyes, I sensed a malevolence. And it was directed at me.

ABOUT THE AUTHOR

Madelyn Sanders will always have a soft spot in her heart for Natchez, Mississippi, the setting of *Darkness at Cottonwood Hall*. She often visited relatives in Natchez when she was a child. Childhood memories helped in the writing of the mystery, and she hopes her Natchez relations will forgive her creation of an antebellum mansion in which to let loose her wild imagination.

Books by Madelyn Sanders

HARLEQUIN INTRIGUE
158—UNDER VENICE
187—SARABANDE

Don't miss any of our special offers. Write to us at the following address for information on our newest releases.

Harlequin Reader Service
P.O. Box 1397, Buffalo, NY 14240
Canadian address: P.O. Box 603,
Fort Erie, Ont. L2A 5X3

Darkness at Cottonwood Hall

Madelyn Sanders

Harlequin Books

TORONTO • NEW YORK • LONDON
AMSTERDAM • PARIS • SYDNEY • HAMBURG
STOCKHOLM • ATHENS • TOKYO • MILAN
MADRID • WARSAW • BUDAPEST • AUCKLAND

Harlequin Intrigue edition published March 1993

ISBN 0-373-22218-1

DARKNESS AT COTTONWOOD HALL

Printed in U.S.A.

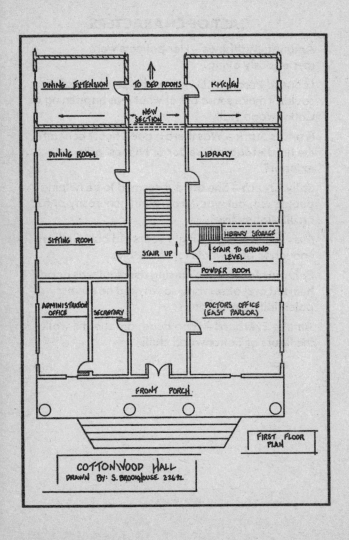

DINING EXTENSION

TO BED ROOMS

KITCHEN

NEW SECTION

DINING ROOM

LIBRARY

SITTING ROOM

LIBRARY STORAGE

STAIR UP

STAIR TO GROUND LEVEL

POWDER ROOM

ADMINISTRATION OFFICE

SECRETARY

DOCTORS OFFICE (EAST PARLOR)

FRONT PORCH

FIRST FLOOR PLAN

COTTONWOOD HALL
DRAWN BY: S. BROOKHOUSE 2-26-92

CAST OF CHARACTERS

Amanda Matthews—Her patients were mysteriously dying.

Leonard Percy, M.D.—Even this psychiatrist couldn't make sense out of what was happening at Cottonwood Hall.

Frances Stark—Was there a good heart beneath the hatchet-faced Director of Nurses' grim exterior?

Sally Creech—She always seemed to be helping people out, but was it from plain generosity or for an ulterior motive?

Miss Lilibet—Eighty-eight years old but still sharp enough to be a whole lot of trouble.

Ephraim Jones—The nursing assistant was good-hearted and observant, so why did he seem potentially threatening?

Amelie Everhard—Long dead, did she still walk the floors of Cottonwood Hall?

Chapter One

I remember, I remember.
I try to forget, but still I remember.... Natchez.
Long, long days of somnolent sun, droning of fat
flies with iridescent eyes upon the heavy, humid
air. And in the smothered afternoons, thunder-
heads massing up in the west, across the river.
The Mississippi River.

I remember magnolias with slick, glossy leaves
and strange pods of blood-red seeds, tall camel-
lia bushes, ancient azaleas as high as my head;
great live oaks gray-bearded with Spanish moss,
and black-barked cypresses with twisted limbs. I
remember the ash trees, the lindens, and the cot-
tonwoods.

Always, always the cottonwoods. I would like
to forget. But I remember Cottonwood Hall.

The fabled, famous Natchez Trace ran from the Tennessee mountains around Nashville westward and
southward until it ended in Natchez, on the banks of

the Mississippi River. It was an old, old, track—in the late 1700s it was already well worn.

In the late 1900s I, too, ran from the Tennessee mountains, ran from death and disappointment. I didn't follow the Natchez Trace, at least not intentionally; but perhaps the old track by some subliminal magnetism compelled my feet. Because I ended up, as had so many before me who had started out in approximately the same place, in Natchez. I had my baby there. Alone. I named her Samantha so that I could call her Sam, after her father, my dead husband. As for my own Mama and Daddy, those proud, stubborn, unyielding parents I'd left back in the Tennessee mountains, the parents who refused to take me back and take me in: I nevermore wanted to hear the sound of their names.

Now Sam was four and the insurance money was running out. I needed a job. That was why I went to Cottonwood Hall.

I left Sam with a sitter and drove toward the south edge of town, at first through quiet residential streets, like mine, that spoke of some mild affluence—neat, small houses with rectangles of green lawn and pecan trees marching politely next to the sidewalks. Then I skirted an older, poorer area where the houses were more like shacks, shabby and weathered gray from lack of paint, their yards haphazardly lush with grass and broken toys, and all kinds of vegetation growing every which way without any regard for order or politeness. Then, suddenly, the road dipped and curved and I left the town behind.

If I had ever been out here before, I didn't recall it. Off to my right I sensed the river. That's how it is in Natchez—you seldom see the river, but you know it's there. The Mississippi has a presence so immense that you feel it. Like God, I've sometimes thought, and then prayed forgiveness for blasphemy. Now my sense of the river was the only thing that kept me from feeling lost, though I had a set of written directions and knew I hadn't strayed.

I kept on driving, I didn't know how long. I seemed to be going back in time, my Honda Civic seemed like an anachronism. I reminded myself that the antebellum mansion, my destination, had survived by being turned into a "rest" home that was really a fancy, discreet, residential treatment center for the mentally ill. That was fortunate for me, since I intended to survive myself by returning to my former profession of psychiatric nurse. Still, when Cottonwood Hall's small sign eventually appeared and showed me where to turn, it might as well have read "You are entering the Twilight Zone."

I was in a long drive, so narrow that surely two cars could not have passed. I slowed to a sedate crawl, mindful of tall trees on either side, their trunks like columns marking a processional way. My car's air conditioner, protesting the slow speed, labored and whined. I turned it off and opened the window. The heavy air of high summer flowed over me, hung on my skin and entered my nostrils, stealing my breath. I gasped and shuddered—whether from the sudden invasion of heat or from some atavistic fear, I did not know.

Around the car, that bubble of civilization which enclosed me, the atmosphere darkened. I heard the rumble of thunder. Of course, I thought, my good sense more or less prevailing, we usually have thunderstorms on summer afternoons. I kept my foot light but steady on the accelerator and went on. On through the ominous purple of a false twilight, thunder rumbling, threatening.

Even before the drive opened up to the great house, before I felt the rising wind that heralds a storm, I heard the moaning, the sighs. The sound filled me with a restless sadness, an apprehensive melancholy. It was the cry of the cottonwoods. I had come at last to Cottonwood Hall.

The great white columns of the portico were an architectural echo of the tall trunks of the cottonwood trees surrounding the house. The Hall held its cottonwoods at bay, seemingly by the sheer grandeur of its presence, creating for itself a broad semicircle of lawn. I stopped the car in the middle of the drive, enthralled.

These great old houses—and there are many of them in Natchez—seem to me as if they have almost earned their own right to exist. As if they didn't need people anymore. Yet, of course, they did. Without the kind attentions of Natchez females of all ages, from three to ninety-three, who twice a year dressed up like their great-great-grandmamas in hoops and crinolines and with brave smiles humiliated themselves for tourist dollars, the mansions would long since have succumbed to decay and taxes.

I could never do that, I thought. I had too much of a mountain woman's stubborn pride. Still, in my own way, I'd fallen under the Natchez spell. I had studied the history and architecture of the great houses in the public library, I had visited those that were open in the off-season, on quiet Sunday afternoons. So it came as no surprise to me that in spite of the ominous surrounding atmosphere, in spite of the eerie moaning and sighing in the tall, swaying trees, I immediately fell in love with Cottonwood Hall.

I did not bother to look for the parking area, I just left my car pulled over to the side of the drive. I had eyes only for the house, which was much, much more impressive than I had imagined. This house didn't beg for tourist dollars; it had, so to speak, chosen to work for a living. In that we were alike, the house and I—I would have made such a choice myself. Fortunately, the transformation into a home for the mentally ill seemed not to have changed the Hall at all. At least, not visually. I approached on foot across the lawn, marveling and analyzing at the same time.

The columned porch extended around the sides of the house. On closer inspection, I realized that the porch and its columns were a later addition, a Greek Revival facade built around an earlier, much older structure. The main body of the house appeared to be Georgian. Its shape suggested a foursquare central hall plan, two stories set upon a high foundation that had probably once been open underneath, but was now enclosed. The Greek Revival addition must have been done about 1850 or so.

I moved back a pace and looked up, to the tops of the tall columns. Their capitals were Ionic, curved like rams' horns. There was, however, one jarring twentieth century note—the porches at second story height were screened. For a moment I frowned, then remembered that this was no showplace, it was a working house and screens were a necessity for porches to be of any use in the buggy climate.

I would have liked to have investigated further, to walk around and see the house from the side, but the cottonwoods—I *supposed* it must be the cottonwoods—gave a banshee wail that startled me. I'd become used to their sighing in the background, and if the thunder had continued during my inspection of the house I hadn't heard it. But now I felt the sudden springing of the wind, in a gust so harsh it was like a body blow. A hard, white glare of lightning almost blinded me.

I ran for my car—I'd left the window down on the driver's side—and when I was halfway there a cracking boom of thunder shook the ground under my feet. The cottonwood trees, greatly disturbed, thrashed their branches overhead.

Oh God, I thought, angry with myself, I should have realized that if I dawdled around gawking at the Hall I'd get caught in the rain! I hurried, not wanting to arrive for my interview looking like a drowned rat. I wrenched open the car door—not an easy feat in the now driving wind—rolled up the window and grabbed my purse and the folder with my résumé off the other seat. I knew I made a great target for lightning bolts as I ran across the empty expanse of lawn. I had almost made it when a sudden feeling of absolute doom gripped me and stopped me in my tracks.

I looked up, my eyes irresistibly drawn to the porch at second story level. The day had turned dark, almost as dark as night. Thick clouds roiled above the Hall, but for a moment the wind dropped, as if in a sudden vacuum. I couldn't breathe, I couldn't move, but I could see. I saw a face, a white face on the porch. The body that must be there to go with the face was invisible, lost in the surrounding darkness. The face stared at me. From that height I could not possibly see its expression, but I felt malevolence directed at me from its burning eyes. I trembled inside; I felt sick to my stomach.

The moment passed. Another white lightning glare illuminated everything, and the face was gone. Vanished! I snatched a breath as the wind caught again, tugging at my skirt, and the first fat drops of rain fell on my own upturned face. I shook my head, not sure what I'd seen, and pushed myself to move. Could I have been almost paralyzed by that, that...what? Vision? What had I really seen? A ghost? And why did I think it had had burning eyes?

I was on the broad sweep of the Hall's steps when the rain came down in earnest. I didn't get too wet, and anyway I was wearing a cotton shirtdress that would dry quickly, and I had my hair pulled back tight from a center part into a bun, the way I had always worn it when I worked. No harm done. I crossed the porch to the handsome front door and rang the bell.

The door was opened by a black man with a young face whose ingenuous expression somehow didn't go with his massive body. He was built like a wrestler and wore whites, like a hospital orderly. He said, "Afternoon, ma'am," and I began to say, "I have an appointment—" when all hell broke loose. Someone screamed somewhere in the house behind him. It was the most awful sound I had ever heard, and in its midst came a tremendous *crack!* of lightning and simultaneous thunder that drowned the scream and shook the Hall to its foundations.

The man spun around and took off at a run across the shaking floor. The scream came again, and so did another bolt of lightning; the sharp smell of ozone slashed through the air. I stepped across the threshold and closed the front door behind me, just as the electricity failed and all the lights went out. In near-total darkness I entered Cottonwood Hall for the first time.

Chapter Two

I stood there in the dark, my back against the door I had just closed. I didn't dare take a step because all around I heard the sound of running feet, and doors being wrenched open and slammed closed. I didn't want to get in the way. I could only stand there and wonder what in the world had happened, who had screamed, and why. The scream seemed to go on and on, but that was only in my head. In reality, the footsteps stopped and the Hall fell eerily silent.

Holding its breath, I thought. But that was not the house, that was me—I was holding my breath. Waiting for something else to happen. For what felt like a very long time, but was probably only a minute or two, nothing did happen. Then another hard, white flash revealed, strobelike, a glimpse of the wide central hallway in which I stood: a couple of straight-backed chairs against the wall, a hunt board, a tall case clock—and darkness again. The following roll of thunder was neither so immediate nor so loud. The storm was moving away, no longer directly overhead.

There were no more screams. I found myself breathing normally, relaxing in relief.

I heard a voice I recognized.

"Amanda, is that you?" It was Sally, my neighbor who had told me about the nursing job here, but she didn't look like her nineteen-year-old self. The flickering candle she held out in front of her cast strange shadows upward on her face. "God!" she said, approaching, "this is so spooky! Not the lights going out, that happens all the time in these storms, but that scream! Did you hear it?"

"Yes," I said. I'd gotten over my initial reaction, and the nurse in me was coming to the fore. "What do you think happened? Someone must have been hurt, maybe I should see if I can help. Come on, show me the way—"

"No," she said, tugging on my arm and holding me back, "I definitely do not think we should do anything except go in the office and wait. Mrs. Stark took off like a bat out of hell—whatever it is, she'll take care of it."

"Not *it*, Sally." I was letting her lead me into the office but I couldn't stop myself from correcting her. "*Her,* or maybe even *him.* I couldn't tell if it was a man or a woman, but that was a person we heard. Not a thing, not an it."

"Yeah, well, you don't know Mrs. Stark yet and I do. I've been her secretary for almost a year now and I can tell you for sure that she didn't get to be the director of this place for nothing. I mean, she really cramps down on security and stuff when something like this happens. You don't want to mess up your chances of getting hired! Oh geez, Amanda.'' She turned to me and in the candle's wavering light her eyes looked wild. "This is really messing up your interview.''

"The heck with my interview,'' I said. "What do you mean, when something like this happens? I was a psychiatric nurse for almost ten years b-before...'' There was so much that had happened *before* that I stumbled on the word and had to push myself past it. "Before I stopped working to move here and have my baby, and I never in my life heard anyone scream like that!''

Sally went behind her desk, sat down, opened a drawer and rummaged around until she came out with a small glass ashtray into which she dripped wax from the tilted, shaking candle. When she was satisfied that she had enough, she twisted the bottom of the candle firmly into the wax. Now the light no longer wavered but lit the small office with a steady if feeble glow.

I didn't think she was going to answer me. I shifted my weight back and forth from one leg to the other, and became aware that I was gripping much too hard, the manila folder that held my résumé. I told myself to lighten up. My grip loosened some, but I was much too disturbed to sit down. "Well, Sally,'' I said, "what did you mean?''

There's nothing like sitting behind a desk to give a person confidence. Sally shrugged. "Nothing special. I just meant in any sort of crisis. I guess this was sort of worse. But geez, Amanda! These patients here do get...upset and stuff. I guess they're entitled—they're *crazy,* you know?''

That wasn't really a question, so I bit my tongue and she went right on. ''Is that your résumé you're holding? Give it to me, and I'll put it on Mrs. Stark's desk. And you better sit down. I'm sure she'll be here in a minute and go ahead with your interview. This hasn't put you off, has it? I mean, you do still want to work here, don't you?''

I just nodded and handed her the folder. I still didn't trust myself to say anything. I sat down as ordered, while Sally went through a door behind and to the left of her desk. A part of my mind registered that a wall must have been put up to partition off this small office from a room that would originally have been much larger, and the other part of my mind was wondering if I knew Sally Creech at all. People who work with the mentally ill did not, in my experience, ever call them crazy. The word crazy is not only pejorative, it's essentially meaningless. Of course, Sally wasn't a trained mental health worker, she was a secretary fresh out of high school, but still! I hadn't realized she could be so insensitive.

She was gone longer than it could possibly have taken to place the folder on her boss's desk, and I supposed she was probably reading my résumé. What the heck, there was nothing personal about it. Sally had taken the candle with her so I was sitting in dark gray gloom, and my mood was beginning to match. I asked myself if I really wanted this job as much as I'd thought I did. The answer to that was easy: yes. I not only wanted the job, I needed it badly because I was almost out of money and I had both myself and my four-year-old daughter to support. I was out of practice, and I'd recently passed the exam to get licensed in Mississippi just by the skin of my teeth....

Footsteps came pounding down the stairs, down the hall, coming in my direction. Sally popped out of the inner room just as an older woman strode through the office door. "Mrs. Stark!" Sally squeaked.

Mrs. Stark, the Administrative Director of Cottonwood Hall, paid no attention to her secretary. She swept the beam of the flashlight she held in her hand full into my face, blinding me. "You're Matthews, the nurse?" she barked.

"Yes," I acknowledged, squinting against the light.

"I need a nurse, right now! You're hired. No time to waste. Sally, you get on the phone and call Dr. Stewart and tell him we need him immediately, it's an emergency! And when you're done with that, call the power company and tell them we need the power back on here! Matthews, you come with me!"

"Mrs. Stark," blurted Sally, all her former confidence vanished, "I can't get Dr. Stewart, he's gone, you remember? I'll have to get that new doctor."

Mrs. Stark was already out the door, with me behind her. She was a very tall, spare woman. Also—to judge from her grip when she'd yanked me up out of the chair—remarkably strong. When she whirled around at Sally's protest, she almost knocked me over. "Well, get him then, whatever his name is. Peevy, Perry, whatever, just get him here!"

"Percy," said Sally.

"You tell Dr. Percy I said if he intends to be staff psychiatrist for Cottonwood Hall he'd better be here in ten minutes or I'll fire his just-out-of-residency booty! Come on, Matthews!''

I liked her. Of course, she shouldn't have said she was hiring me on the spot like that, without seeing my résumé or checking my references or anything. I could have been Jack the Ripper in drag for all she knew. But I liked her style.

"Been out of nursing for a while, have you Matthews? So Sally tells me," she said over her shoulder as she led the way at a brisk pace up the stairs.

"Yes," I said. I was excited, anticipating a kind of action I hadn't been a part of in a long time. I hadn't realized until this moment how much I'd missed it.

"Well, I hope you can still remember a thing or two. I used to be a nurse myself but that was a long time ago, and this medpool RN we've got turns out to have about as much psychiatric nursing experience as a cockroach. I warn you, Matthews—what's your first name?" At the top of the stairs she whirled around and blinded me with the flashlight again.

"Amanda," I said.

"I warn you, Amanda Matthews, if you turn out to be no good, I'll fire your booty just as quick as I hired you! Now let's go to work!"

"Fair enough," I said, scrambling up the remaining step to follow behind her tall, dark-suited figure silhouetted against its bobbing flashlight beam. I was aware of polished floors, high ceilings, shadowy figures hanging back in doorways, tall windows at the end of the wide hallway down which we walked, and thunder still rumbling in the distance.

At the last door before the windows Mrs. Stark stopped. Her harsh voice was moderated into low, gravelly tones. "Patient's in here. A woman, Belinda Stokes, age 42, has bipolar disorder—what they used to call manic-depression. She's been on the downside ever since she came here about six months ago. Medpool nurse tells me Doc Stewart couldn't get her regulated on lithium carbonate, but there's no explanation for what happened to her a few minutes ago. I don't know what's going on here. You take a look, Matthews. Be careful, now. Belinda clawed the medpool nurse in the face, and she won't let Jones— he's the male nursing assistant—near her. Of course, he could overpower her if necessary, but I'd rather not have to do that. She hisses and spits at me. Maybe you'll have better luck."

"Has she, has Belinda," I reminded myself that psychiatric patients, just like everybody else in the world, respond better when called by their own names, "been violent before?"

"Not since coming to us. I don't know about before that. I haven't exactly had time to sit down and read the medical history in her chart."

I nodded, took the flashlight and partially shielded it with my fingers. Then I entered the room. Its proportions were spacious and there were two large windows opposite the door. As my eyes adjusted to the dim light—it was a shade lighter here than in the hallway—I quickly noted the placement of furniture. I saw the big, white-garbed nursing assistant over to my right, but I did not see Belinda.

I took a couple of cautious steps forward, noticing a soft rug underfoot. Then I saw her. She was crouched, hiding, on the far side of a double bed. A large, four-poster bed. In spite of the desperate situation, the room surprised me. Its furnishings were more like a bed-and-breakfast than any mental care facility I'd ever seen.

"Hi, Belinda," I said, keeping my voice soft. "My name's Amanda. I'm new here."

So far, so good. Her head lifted in an effort to get a better look at me. I couldn't see her well, either. I could only tell that her face was very white and her hair was long, tangled and dark with lighter streaks that would probably prove to be gray when there was more light to see by.

"Why don't we both sit on the bed?" I suggested. "That way we could see each other better, and I'd like to talk to you." I approached the bed. Belinda began to make a high, keening sound. Please, God, I prayed, don't let her scream again! I sat gingerly on the very edge of the bed. She keened louder and threw herself down on the floor so that I could no longer see her.

Jones, the nursing assistant, walked across the room. He circled the bed, giving it a wide berth, then came back to me and reported in a voice so low it was almost a whisper, "She's just lying there. She had a hallucination, that's what was wrong with her. That temporary nurse just scared her, made her worse, that's why she scratched her like that. But now, I don't know... You're a nurse, you know about people like Miss Stokes?"

"I'm a nurse, I know a little," I murmured.

"Well, you better come around here then and take a look."

I slipped off the bed and walked around, with Jones, to the other side. From the corner of my eye I saw Mrs. Stark standing in the doorway.

Belinda Stokes lay faceup in a rigid posture on the floor between the bed and the wall, her head toward the foot of the bed. Her eyes were wide open and so was her mouth, as if she were trying to scream again but no sound would come.

"Hold the flashlight," I said to Jones as I handed it to him, "so that it shines near her, but not on her. I need to see better." He did as requested.

There was not enough room for me to kneel beside the woman, so I had to make do with kneeling at her head. I didn't like this; it meant that I was looking at her upside down and that, if she could see me at all, she saw me upside down, too. It was a kind of visual distortion, and if she'd already had a hallucination... Well, it couldn't be helped.

"Belinda!" I said sharply. "Belinda Stokes!" No response. Not even the flicker of an eyelid. I clapped my hands together with an abrupt crack, only inches in front of her face. The sudden loud sound startled me even though I was the one doing it, but Belinda's face remained a mask. Her body didn't move, didn't even twitch.

"She dead?" asked Jones in an awed voice.

I had never thought this woman was faking, but as I reached out to feel for a pulse at the carotid site on the side of her neck, I automatically braced myself for a sudden clawing grasp at my flesh. It didn't happen.

Her pulse was there, regular but faint and too slow. "No, she's not dead," I said to Jones. I leaned over Belinda, took her wrist in my hand and raised her arm. There was some rigidity, but not as much as I'd expected.

Mrs. Stark had come into the room and now she stretched out her tall body across the bed, the better to see Belinda Stokes lying on the floor and me bending over her. "She gone catatonic?" she asked.

"No," I replied. "That's what I thought, but she isn't." If she had been catatonic her arm would have been so stiff that it would have remained in the air when I let go. I could have demonstrated the absence of catatonia by simply dropping Belinda's arm, but it seemed an unnecessary indignity. I folded her arm at her waist instead and said, "You see, if she was catatonic her limbs would be too rigid to fold this way. I haven't counted her respirations, but her pulse is weak and much too slow."

"Hmm," said Mrs. Stark. I looked over at her. Her chin rested on the edge of the bed, and for the first time I saw her face clearly. She was probably about sixty. I'd heard of women described as hatchet-faced but I'd never actually seen one before. Mrs. Stark had a face as severe and clean of feature as the blade of an axe. There was not a hint of softness anywhere in that visage. Yet I sensed she was not unkind, and the instinct most nurses have about other professionals told me she had once been a good nurse. Her peculiar position on the bed did not make her a bit less formidable.

"I think," I said carefully, "that if the doctor doesn't get here within the next couple of minutes, we should go ahead and call an ambulance. I have no idea what caused it, but Belinda Stokes is in a coma."

"I agree," said Mrs. Stark. "Good work, Amanda Matthews."

"I didn't do anything," I said, frustrated. "As soon as I got into the room she keeled over, there wasn't time to do anything!"

Mrs. Stark rolled to her feet and stood to her considerable height. "Never argue when somebody says you've done good work, Amanda, especially if it's me who says so. My first name's Frances and you can call me Frances when you feel like it. Unless I find out from your references that you've done something terrible, like killing your grandmother, you can stay."

She held out her hand and I shook it. "Thanks, Frances," I said, and at that moment the electricity was restored. We were still blinking at each other when the doctor arrived.

"That's Dr. Leonard Percy," said Frances in her harsh low voice. "He's still wet behind the ears, and so full of himself that he probably thinks he made the lights come on!"

Chapter Three

He came loping up the hall so rapidly that his knee-length white doctor's coat flapped out behind him. As he got closer I saw, in a way, what Frances Stark meant about Dr. Leonard Percy being wet behind the ears. He had sandy blond hair that was a little too long and fell down over one eye, and a face like a big, friendly kid. But he wasn't a kid—he had too many lines in his face for youth, and all of them turned upward as if he smiled a lot. Sure enough, as he joined us that friendly face lit up in a grin.

His grin quickly faded, though, when Frances explained about Belinda Stokes. She finished with a nod at me, "This is Amanda Matthews, the new day nurse. Matthews, stay with the doctor. Jones, you come on with me in case I need help—we've got to get the rest of these people settled down."

We'd been standing in a clump in the doorway of Belinda's room. Now Dr. Percy stepped in, looked around and back over his shoulder at me. "Where's the patient?"

"On the other side of the bed," I said softly, leading the way. "Here. On the floor."

"Oh, Lord," he said, going down on his knees to start his examination. I looked around for the chart so that I could make notes of what he said, and found it on top of a four-drawer chest. But I didn't have a pen—after all, I hadn't come prepared to go right to work, and I'd left my purse in Stark's office downstairs. So I clutched the chart to my chest and watched and listened intently.

I liked what I saw: a doctor who was swift, sure and gentle. Leonard Percy was a big man but not bulky. Crowded in the small space beside the bed, his long legs were folded up like a grasshopper's. He finished his palpations and said without looking up, "There's some mild rigidity. No bruises or contusions. Skin temp abnormally cool."

I committed this to memory without comment. Dr. Percy wrestled a stethoscope out of his jacket pocket, hooked the instrument in his ears and, in a gesture that immediately endeared him to me, unconsciously warmed it for a moment between the palms of his big hands before he placed it on Belinda's chest. His sandy hair fell over his forehead as he bent his head to listen. In the dead quiet of the room I picked out Belinda's shallow respirations and counted, looking at the second hand on my watch. Respiration was on the low side of normal range. Drug overdose? I wondered, and opened the chart.

All medical charts follow the same general format. This one was remarkably thin, as if nothing much worth writing down had ever happened to Belinda

Stokes. Her only prescribed medication was lithium. As I was mentally retrieving the symptoms of lithium overdose, Dr. Percy unfolded himself and stepped over the patient, out of the confined space between bed and wall. He whipped his head around impatiently, ran a hand through his hair and muttered, "Confound it!"

"I'm sorry?" I didn't know what he wanted.

"Aren't there any telephones in these rooms? Never mind, I'll call from Dr. Stewart's office. I mean, *my* office. What a way to start a new job! This patient belongs in the hospital. Stay with her, Miz Matthews, while I make the call."

"Of course." I laid her chart on the bed and sat on the floor by poor Belinda's head. Dr. Percy must have closed her eyes because they were closed now, but her mouth was still open, locked in that soundless scream. I smoothed her hair as best I could, but it was hard to look at her. Even with her eyes closed she looked both frightened and frightening. I looked away. This was no lithium overdose. I might have been away from nursing for five years, but I remembered the symptoms: excessive thirst, twitching, exaggerated muscular reactions, confusion, difficulty speaking, and if it got far enough, apathy. Apathy before coma, though I'd never seen it get that far. This woman had certainly not been apathetic before becoming comatose!

Dr. Percy came back. "Ambulance is on its way. Now, while we're waiting I'd appreciate you telling me everything you know about how this happened."

I stood up, dusting my skirt and feeling inadequate. "I can only tell you what the orderly, Jones, told me when I came into the room. Mrs. Stark wanted me to try to calm Miss Stokes. I wasn't the nurse on duty.''

"You weren't? Then where is she?"

"I don't know, I haven't seen her. She's a temporary, hired from the Med Pool." I moved toward the door. "If you don't mind, I'd prefer that we talk in the hall."

When we'd moved outside the room I explained, "I know we think Belinda Stokes is in a coma, but still I'd rather we didn't talk about her right in front of her like that. If you don't mind, Dr. Percy."

"Not at all. In fact, I agree with you. We don't know whether people who appear to be unconscious can hear or not. I appreciate your sensitivity. And by the way, since we're going to be working together, I prefer first names. Mine's Len. And you're—Amanda?"

"Amanda," I confirmed, smiling. So far I'd seen signs of him being gentle, considerate, and now unpretentious—I liked him better all the time. "Well, to get back to the little I know of what happened, apparently Belinda Stokes had some sort of hallucination that frightened her. I do know she screamed. I heard the scream—I was downstairs. She sounded absolutely terrified. Mrs. Stark said she scratched the medpool nurse in the face; Jones said she did it because the nurse scared her, on top of whatever hallucination it was she had. It was all very confused, because of the thunderstorm. All the lights went out. When I came into this room it was almost totally dark, I had just a flashlight, and Jones was standing over there, by the chest of drawers. Belinda was hiding behind the bed and she looked—well, I can't find a clinical word for it, but she was wide-eyed, wild-looking. I sat down on the bed and asked her to join me, sit and talk with me.''

"That was sensible. Calming.''

"I hoped so, but she started making this high-pitched sort of sound. I've been a psychiatric nurse for a lot of years, but I never heard anyone make that kind of sound before. It was eerie, sort of the vocal equivalent of fingernails on a blackboard.''

"Ugh! Go on.''

"That's all. She made the high-pitched noise and then she collapsed, right where she is now. I checked her, but I didn't move her. She was rigid, but not catatonic. Her pulse was regular but slow. I didn't count her respirations then but I did just now when you were examining her, and they were in the low-normal range.''

Len nodded. "The only thing I can add to that is that her lungs are clear. She's in no immediate danger but I still want her in the hospital.''

"Oh, I could add a lot to that, but I don't think you'd believe me. Nobody ever believes me,'' said a thin, sweet voice. Without a hint of complaint, just a simple statement of fact.

I saw Len smile, a generous smile that crinkled his cheeks near his eyes, and I turned to look behind me. I had to look down before I saw the elderly woman, she was so tiny.

"I'm Miss Elizabeth Anne Bowe, but everybody calls me Lilibet. All my life—and that's a long, long eighty-eight years of it—I've been called Lilibet,'' she said. ''And who are you?''

Len bowed to her, a courtly dip of head and shoulders that was in deference to her age and in keeping with the way she was dressed. She wore pale blue lace in an elegant style that used to be called a tea dress, the skirt falling in handkerchief points to just above birdthin ankles clad in white stockings, small feet in white shoes. Around her fragile neck she had draped a ransom in pearls, loops and loops of them spilling down her flat chest almost to her waist. Age had whitened her hair and thinned her skin to translucence, but she still had a rosebud of mouth and a gleam in eyes that were a darker blue than her dress.

Len said, ''We've met, Miss Lilibet. I'm Dr. Percy. Perhaps you don't remember, but Dr. Stewart introduced us a couple of weeks ago. I'm the one who's taking his place on staff here at Cottonwood Hall.''

She looked him up and down, very thoroughly. Then she said, ''I don't remember. I have Alzheimer's, you know. That's why I'm here.'' She subjected me to the same scrutiny and pronounced, ''You're a pretty girl. I'm sure I'd remember you, you have such lovely skin. Good skin is a thing to be prized, you know.'' I blushed, which only encouraged her. ''And you color up quite nicely, too, so you must have a modest nature. What's your name, dear?''

''I'm Amanda Matthews. Thank you for the compliments. I'm a new nurse here. I expect I'll be seeing a lot of you from now on, Miss Lilibet.''

At that point the ambulance team arrived, rushing up the stairs with their equipment. Behind them came Jones and a nurse in whites. The absent medpool temporary, no doubt. I moved back well out of the way and Miss Lilibet moved with me. Her eyes were bright. She didn't seem to be missing a thing, and I thought that if she did have Alzheimer's disease, it couldn't be far advanced. At least at this moment, Miss Lilibet was very much in touch with reality.

She touched my arm to get my attention. "I do know what happened to poor Belinda."

"You do? Were you here before the lights went out?"

"I was at the other end of the hall." She pointed and I looked. That would be the front of the house. At the far reach of gleaming hardwood floor and creamy plastered walls punctuated with doors to the rooms on either side, and an occasional chair or chest, there was a pair of multipaned French doors. "I wanted to go out onto the porch, to watch the storm come. I just love storms, don't you?"

I didn't particularly, but because she expected it I said, "Oh yes. Especially in summer."

Miss Lilibet smiled, and a faraway look came into her eyes. "We had a porch swing, and I'd sit out there and swing back and forth and watch the sky get all dark, and feel the air get all heavy and still. It was so exciting! I always loved to watch the storms come. And when a storm's coming, it's best to be out on the porch, you know."

"Why's that?"

"Why, because in these big old houses—like my house and this one—that's when the ghosts walk. Thunderstorms bring them out specially. Of course they walk at night, too, but you know how the light gets that sort of strange quality just before a thunderstorm? The ghosts like that, it brings them out."

She was giving me goose pimples. "Oh," I said.

Miss Lilibet nodded gravely. "That's what scared Belinda. She saw the ghost, and it made her scream."

I tried to shut out the memory but I couldn't. The vision of a white face, disembodied, up on the porch of Cottonwood Hall was replayed in my mind. Against my better judgment I asked, "Did you see the ghost yourself, today, out on the porch?"

"No dear, I couldn't go out on the porch. They had the doors locked. I ask them not to do that because I like to go out there. I like to walk, you see I get so stiff in my joints and the walking helps. I'm curious, too, and from the porch I can see who comes and goes. I like to know what's going on in this place. Even if it isn't much of a place. Now my old house, it's called Bowebelle up on Lake Washington north of here at Glen Allan, maybe you know it? That was a real place...."

She went on, rambling now, and I let myself be distracted by the orderly commotion that was going on in Belinda Stokes's room. Lilibet and I had backed up against the tall window at our end of the hall. The door of the room across from Belinda's, on our left, was closed. Through Belinda's open door I could hear the tone of Len's voice, but not his words, and swishing sounds that were the lifting of a body onto the folding stretcher brought by the ambulance team, then the crisp, crunching sound of Velcro straps sealed into place. In a moment, the team came through the door bearing the unconscious body of Belinda Stokes.

Lilibet fell silent and took a couple of little steps forward. I stayed at her side. She whispered, "She's not dead, is she?"

"No, but she's in a coma. They're taking her to the hospital where they can monitor her and do some tests to find out what happened to her."

"That's right," said Len, coming to join us.

"I told you." Lilibet looked up at me and then at Len, a tiny frown line between her white eyebrows. "I know what happened. She saw the ghost, and it scared her!"

Len quirked one eyebrow and his mouth also quirked upward on that same side. He said nothing, but opened Belinda's chart and began to write in it.

I returned my attention to Lilibet. "If you didn't see this ghost yourself, Miss Lilibet, then why do you think Belinda Stokes saw it? How can you be so sure that's what made her scream?"

She pulled her shoulders back and drew herself to her full height—all of about four foot eleven. "Because I know there's a ghost of a woman in this house. I've seen her with my own eyes, at night. You mark my words, it was the ghost that scared poor Belinda!"

I looked at Len and he glanced up at me over the top of the chart. He was amused, he didn't believe her. I didn't think I believed her, either, but my mind wasn't closed on the subject of ghosts. In the mountains where I grew up there were plenty of ghost stories and

I'd always felt a kind of wary respect for the possibility of their existence.

Miss Lilibet's voice lost its ring of conviction and took on the wispy tones of memory. "We have a ghost at home, at Bowebelle. Such a lovely place, Bowebelle. I do miss it so, but it was really too big for me, too much for me all by myself. It's really better for me here...." She wandered off, no longer aware of us, her voice trailing behind her softer and softer, "But dear Bowebelle, I do miss it so...."

I watched Miss Lilibet disappear down the stairs, her hand tiny and very white on the dark mahogany of the banister. "My goodness!" I said when she was gone.

"She's a character, all right! Now to get back to our case. Jones says hallucination, Miss Lilibet says it was a ghost, that young nurse, I forget her name, doesn't say anything and seems to know less. The chart tells me nothing to suggest an episode of this sort. It says she was stabilized, all her vital signs normal for the past weeks. So your educated guess is as good as mine at this point. What do you think, Amanda?"

I tried for clincial consideration but I simply did not know enough for that. And besides, other things—intuition, feelings, Len Percy's irresistibly friendly face—got in the way. Finally I said, "I don't know. It's a mystery."

Chapter Four

"Mommy, Mommy!" My four-year-old daughter Sam came running to meet me, banging the back door screen behind her.

"Hi, sweetie!" I got out of the car and caught her up in my arms, loving as always the fresh smell and the silkiness of her hair, the softness of her skin.

My Samantha was a constant reminder of her father, Sam Matthews. I hadn't known, when she was born and I named her for him, that she'd grow to look so much like him: red-brown hair, snub nose, wide mouth, a tendency to freckle. But she had my dark brown eyes—Sam's eyes had been hazel green. And she was more like me in temperament: reserved, disinclined to take risks, especially physical risks. Perhaps she'd picked that up from me and would have been more of a risk taker if her father had been alive to help bring her up. Sam Matthews had been a helicopter pilot in the Army, a born daredevil, afraid of nothing and no one. But that wasn't what got him killed. A mechanical malfunction, they said. I'd been an Army nurse, patching up wounds both physical and psychological. But after the crash I never got the chance to patch up my Sam.

I gave my little Sam a squeeze. I knew I'd been an overprotective mother. Now it was time to begin to let go a little.

She wriggled out of my hug, bouncing with excitement. "Did you get the job, Mommy?"

"Yes, sweetie, I did. I start the day after tomorrow."

"Oh, goody!" She bounced across the grass toward the back door. "Now I get to go to school all day, every day! Just like the big children!"

I smiled. "That's right, sweetheart." But I felt a sudden ache, a heaviness near my heart. Anticipating that I would need to go back to work soon, in the spring I'd enrolled my daughter in a preschool program, mornings only, three days a week as a kind of transition. The same preschool had a full day-care program.

Fortunately for both of us, Sam had loved school from the very start. The teachers were good, letting the children go at their own pace in their learning and play. They didn't push Sam to do the physical things like climbing on the outdoor equipment until she was ready, nor did they hold her back from her passionate desire to learn to read. I was the one who needed the transition, not my precocious daughter. I was the one who faced starting a new job with a sense of loss.

Sam was growing up. Life goes on, I thought as I followed her through the back door and opened my purse to pay the baby-sitter. It will be interesting, I told myself, it will be good for both of us. But I felt uneasy.

TWO MORNINGS LATER my stomach was full of butterflies.

"You look nice in your uniform, Mommy," said Sam. She sat on the edge of my bed, swinging her short legs back and forth as she watched me fix my hair. "I wish I had a uniform. Why don't children have uniforms to wear to school?"

If I told her that in some places children did wear school uniforms, she would immediately want to go there. So I asked instead, "If you had a uniform, what would you want it to look like?"

Sam thought about this. I glanced at her over my shoulder. I'd braided her thick, curly auburn hair and tied the braids at the ends with blue bows that matched her T-shirt. She also wore jeans and red sneakers. Sam said, "White is nice for nurses, but it's not very practical for children because it's so easy to get dirty."

I smiled. She reasoned pretty well for a four-year-old. "That's true," I said, smiling as I began to wind my long hair into a coil.

"I guess blue would be okay," said Sam, looking down at her shirt, "but blue is kind of boring."

"Boring" was a word she'd learned from her teenage baby-sitter the day I'd gone to Cottonwood Hall. For the past two days Sam had labeled a number of things boring, to my amusement—my daughter had only the vaguest concept of "boring."

"I think blue is a nice color," I said. "I like it very much, myself."

"Green is better," said Sam seriously. "Green and yellow would be very, very good for a uniform. If I ever got to have a uniform to wear to school. But when I grow up I want a white one just like yours, Mommy. And white shoes and stockings, too. I want to be a nurse when I grow up. Can I hold your gold pin until you have to put it on?"

"It's 'may I,' and yes you may." I handed her my graduate nursing pin and bit back my suggestion that she might prefer to be a doctor. Pushing her would have just as detrimental an effect on her development as my own parents' holding me back had on mine. I'd rebelled. I'd won my freedom but lost the love of my mother and father. I didn't want anything to lose me Sam's love, not ever.

She was saying, "And when I grow up I want my hair to be long and straight and black, just like yours. But it won't be, will it? My hair will always be curly and red. I like your hair better when you wear it down, Mommy."

"I can't leave my hair down when I'm working, honey." I stuck in the final pin to hold the heavy coiled knot at the back of my head, then turned my head back and forth to be sure it would stay. A touch of blusher on my cheeks, and I'd be ready. If only the butterflies would settle down!

"Why can't you?"

"Because it's not neat, and nurses are supposed to be neat." I held out my hand for Sam to return my pin and when she did, I pinned it to my lapel. The uniform was new, and in it I did look neat. But I felt strange, almost sick to my stomach. I mustn't let my daughter see that. I pasted a smile on my face. "Come on, it's time to go!"

Sam slid off the bed and grabbed my hand, her little fingers pulling me along. "Oh wow, this is great!" she said.

MY NEXT TWO DAYS were a blur of learning new people and a new routine. Cottonwood Hall was very, very different from the Army psychiatric hospitals I'd worked in before. "We try to keep a relaxed, home-like atmosphere here," Frances Stark said, "and in keeping with that we call our people here *residents,* not patients."

This seemed reasonable, even positive, but it was hard for me. As soon as I put on that white uniform I automatically thought of those who needed me as patients. And no matter how much I might approve of the concept of a homelike atmosphere, this was too relaxed to meet my professional standards. I had to keep reminding myself that I'd been trained by the military to work in military hospitals, so my standards were bound to be different. That didn't necessarily mean mine were right, and Cottonwood Hall's were wrong. Did it?

Because of the crisis I'd walked into that first day, and because Mrs. Stark—I couldn't quite think of her as Frances yet—had so highly approved of the way I'd handled myself in the crisis, she'd skipped the usual job interview. I'd been relieved at the time, but I'd forgotten that one reason for job interviews is for the applicant to make judgments, too. I hadn't even seen the whole layout of the place before I'd accepted the job, nor had I asked about essential things like patient-to-staff ratio. I should have. Too late I discovered that the emphasis at Cottonwood Hall was on material luxuries, not patient care. As much as I needed the job, as much as I loved and enjoyed being in the beautiful old house, that bothered me.

There were eighteen residents, all in single rooms. The largest, most elegant rooms were those in the main part of the house, six of which were on the second floor. At the moment, only five were occupied, because Belinda Stokes's room was empty. She was still in the hospital, still in a coma, her condition unchanged—and as far as I knew, still unexplained. Twelve more residents were lodged in twelve rooms of an addition that had been extended from the kitchen ell at the back of the house. For these eighteen people there was only one registered nurse per shift, and one nursing assistant. Jones, whose first name was Ephraim, told me that all the nursing assistants were male. For safety's sake he'd said, "in case we have to restrain people."

On the day shift there was also a housekeeper, a small, wiry black woman who had the old-fashioned servant's attitude that she should be seldom seen and never heard, and a cook whom I met on my tour through the kitchen and never saw again. Both these women did their jobs extraordinarily well. The food was more than delicious, it was sumptuous, and the house was a paragon of cleanliness. Nevertheless, it wasn't much staff to take care of seriously mentally ill people with diagnoses that ran the gamut from schizophrenia to depression.

Frances Stark seemed to stay in her office all the time. I learned that Len Percy, as staff psychiatrist, kept office hours at Cottonwood Hall only once a week. Of course, he was always on call for emergencies. Sally Creech was more accessible. In fact, she was all over the place at all hours, delivering messages, running errands and being generally friendly with the residents. I supposed this was fine even though she had no training, and I never knew when I was going to bump into her. At any rate, if I wanted to learn more about Cottonwood Hall, I soon saw that it would have to be from Sally.

On my second day at the new job I asked Sally to join me for lunch. We met in the dining room, which was just beyond the kitchen in the new wing—the original dining room of the main house was now a formal parlor where the patients could see family and visitors. The two front rooms that had originally been parlors were both offices now—the partitioned one shared by Sally and Mrs. Stark, and the second one was the doctor's—Len's. The remaining ground floor rooms in the old part of the house, the library and the music room, were both still intact for the residents to use.

At 1:15, Sally and I had the dining room to ourselves. The house was quiet because the residents were supposed to rest from one to three. Lunch was crab Newburg over toast points or rice, tiny green peas, Bibb lettuce salad, fresh-baked croissants, a compote of pears, and a cake with chocolate butter frosting—all set out in silver serving dishes upon a walnut sideboard. The meal had been equally elegant the day before.

As I served myself I remarked to Sally, "If the food's always this rich, not to mention this good, I'm going to have to be careful! I could gain weight just looking at all this!"

"Oh, don't I know it!" said Sally, rolling her eyes. "But you can use the exercise room after you get off work. They don't mind, all that stuff's just sitting there and the residents hardly ever use any of it. I do, that's how I can eat like this—" she lifted a fork dripping with creamy crab Newburg, "and not get tubby."

"Exercise room?"

"Yeah. Haven't you seen it?"

"Not yet." I was puzzled. "But I went all over the house yesterday."

"Oh, it's the greatest! There's just about everything. Except no Nautilus machines. There's a treadmill and a stationary bike and mirrors and mats and a Jacuzzi and a sauna. I use the sauna every night—I just sweat the calories off."

I looked across the table at Sally as if I were seeing her for the first time. And in a way, I was. A year ago, when she'd first moved in next door to me, she'd had a kind of skinny raw-bonedness about her, which I'd put down to her youth and the fact that she'd just moved to town from out in the country. I doubt she'd have known a Nautilus or a sauna from a hole in the ground then.

She had changed so gradually that I hadn't really noticed before. Sally wasn't skinny anymore, she'd ripened. And she'd lightened her hair. The once mousy

Sally was now a luscious young blonde. I felt dark and dowdy by comparison, an old, old thirty-four, a single mother whose life was over almost before it had begun.

I mentally shook myself and recalled the reason I'd asked Sally to join me. She'd given me an opening, and I intended to take advantage of it. "Where is this exercise room, Sally?"

"It's downstairs in the basement. Except it isn't really a basement. I guess you have to call it the ground floor."

"Uh-huh. You probably know, Sally, that the old houses were often built open underneath—that way if the river flooded, there would be less damage. They used the ground floor level for storage, and sometimes they would drive their carriages right in under the house and go up an inside stairway."

"No, I never knew that. It's interesting, Amanda, like a history lesson."

I ate a few more bites and then said offhandedly, "Well anyway, I'm impressed that there would be an exercise facility in a place like Cottonwood Hall. But to tell you the truth, I'm a little concerned, too, because we don't have enough staff to assign someone to supervise it. I suppose it's kept locked?"

"Of course not. How could anybody use it if it was locked?" She dismissed my concerns with a wave of her fork. Her eyes were shining. "Didn't I tell you, Amanda? Didn't I tell you what a great place this is?"

"Yes, you did, but still I had no idea. I thought you just meant because it's one of the Natchez antebellum homes, the architecture and all that. I had no idea the whole operation would be so, so—'' for a moment I was at a loss for words ''—luxurious. To tell you the truth, it almost makes me uncomfortable.''

''Nothing but the best for the Cypress Group!'' Sally declared, starting on a huge piece of chocolate layer cake.

''The Cypress Group?''

''Sure. They're the real owners. See, it's a chain, they have rest homes like this one all over the South. They buy up old mansions nobody can afford to keep up anymore and turn them into rest homes like this one.''

''Sally, this isn't a rest home. This is a facility for the mentally ill.''

''Well, I know that's right, the people here are crazy and everything, but it's like they don't want to call it that because there's a sti—uh, a whatchacallit—''

''A stigma?''

''Yeah, a stigma attached to it.'' She leaned over the table and said in a near whisper, ''The people here, the residents I mean, they're really, really rich, you know? I mean these people have some serious money! I know because I do all the bills. I mean it's just incredible, and they're so rich they don't even have to have health insurance or anything. Most of them have these trusts that just pay whatever you bill them. It's amazing!''

''I see. So that's how we get all these expensive extras, like the food and the antique furniture and the exercise room and fresh flowers every day....''

''Aren't the flowers really something? Of course they don't come from a regular florist, there's a woman who brings them from the farmers' market. I just love taking the flowers around, it's almost my favorite part of my job.''

"Um-hmm.'' I thought I would probe a little further, but carefully. "On the other hand, considering all the luxuries, the staff seems small...."

"That's why our salaries are so good!''

Perhaps my salary was higher than I would have made elsewhere in the area. I didn't know, though it didn't seem so to me. But to be fair, the only basis I had for comparison was what I'd made five years ago in an Army hospital in a northeastern state.

"We're lucky,'' Sally insisted. She was looking at me a little oddly, so I managed a smile and a nod. She seemed relieved, and gave forth one final burst of praise. "All the residents here are used to living this way, it's how they lived before they came here and how they'd live if they were able to be in their own homes. So we make it like that for them, to them this *is* a homelike atmosphere.''

That sounded like the party line, and Sally had swallowed it, hook, sinker and all—with stars in her eyes.

SATURDAY CAME. I'd only worked two days and already I was exhausted, looking forward to the weekend. I knew I was lucky not to have to work alternating weekends, not to mention alternating shifts; either would have been virtually impossible for me with Sam. Perhaps I should just forget my qualms and enjoy the perks of working in a rest home for the rich of infirm mind.

Sam was certainly enjoying our new schedule. She declared that being in school all day made her feel "mature," and the only thing she didn't like about it was naps. Only babies took naps. I smiled at that, thinking, *Only babies and exhausted mothers.* My active and ever-curious daughter had given up her nap by the time she was two. I used to take her, and a basketful of toys, into my bedroom with me and lock the door while I napped and Sam played on the floor beside my bed.

I tousled her hair and asked, "Where did you learn that word, *mature?*"

"From the mother-helper. She told the teacher I was very mature for my age, and I heard her."

"You seem to have understood what it meant."

Sam nodded. "It means like old. Like I'm old for my age. That's good, isn't it? I thought so, it felt good to me."

I laughed. Oh, the joys of youth! "It feels good until you really are mature, and then you're not so sure anymore."

Sam put her little fists on her hips and cocked her head to one side. "Sometimes, Mommy, I just don't understand you!"

I laughed again. The stance, along with the words, she got straight from me. "Never mind, sweetheart. You can go outside and play. Just be sure you stay in the backyard. Don't go out on the sidewalk or anywhere near the street."

"I won't."

I knew she wouldn't. She was a very responsible child and indeed she was mature for her age. I told myself again—for about the millionth time, it seemed—that she and I had been too close in the past and she needed the experiences that full-time daycare would bring.

The truth was, I felt a little depressed. Sad. Down. I was being forced to begin a new life, and I wasn't anywhere near as ready for it as Sam obviously was.

I wouldn't feel sorry for myself, I vowed. But I could allow myself to rest for just a few minutes. No harm in that, resting. I was sitting at the kitchen table, and I put my head down on my folded arms.

The telephone rang. It nearly startled me out of my wits—I'd actually fallen asleep! I scrambled up to answer it, and on my way looked out of the window over the sink. Yes, Sam was there playing right where she should be, under a tree in the backyard. I picked up the phone.

"Hello."

"Hi. This is Len Percy. I hope I didn't catch you at a bad time."

"No. I just had to check on my daughter before I answered. She's outside."

There was a silence on the other end of the line that gave me a sinking feeling. I'd experienced this kind of reaction before from men who'd seemed interested in me, but as soon as they knew I had a child the interest vanished. But when he finally said something, Len surprised me.

"I didn't know you had a daughter." His tone of voice was different than I had expected.

"Her name's Samantha. I call her Sam. She's four."

"That's great! Uh, listen Amanda, I hope you don't mind me calling like this. I realize you're not in the phone book. I had to look in the office records to get your number."

"No, it's all right." I'd kept an unlisted number since coming to Natchez so that my parents couldn't call me—I had figured it was better to know that they couldn't call than to wait and hope for a call that would never come.

"Well, it may not be all right once you hear what I wanted. I was hoping you could meet me for dinner. I wanted to talk to you about something. I didn't realize you were married and had a family—you'll be wanting to spend your weekend with them."

Ah. The note of carefulness in his voice made me think of his friendly face with all its smile lines and ready grin, and the inherent thoughtfulness that had caused him to warm a stethoscope before putting it to the skin of a comatose woman. I found myself smiling as I said gently, "I'm not exactly married, Len. I've been a widow since before Sam was born. But—" I started to get cold feet. "I can't—"

He jumped right in. "If you can't make it tonight, I understand. I know it's short notice. But Amanda, I really do want to talk to you. How about tomorrow?"

I took a deep breath for courage and suggested, "How about brunch?" Bright daylight on a summer Sunday should be safe enough. And besides, this didn't sound purely social, it sounded like he had something on his mind. Belinda Stokes maybe, Cottonwood Hall?

Len was saying, "That's a good idea. I hear the Melrose Inn does a terrific Sunday brunch. What time's good for you?"

"Around noon?"

"Noon it is. I have your address here—I got it when I got the phone number. I'll come for you."

"No," I said hastily, "I'll meet you. I know the Melrose Inn. Better give me your number, though, in case I can't get a baby-sitter. If I don't call, I'll be there at noon."

"Fine. I'm looking forward to it."

"Me too. Thanks, Len."

IN FACT, the one teenager I trusted to be my regular baby-sitter was busy. I'd never bothered to get a backup. I seldom really wanted to go out anyway, so if the sitter was busy I'd always cancelled.

This time I surprised myself. I walked across the yard and asked Sally Creech to stay with Sam so that I could have brunch with a friend. Sally said she would.

When I was back in the house again, I noticed I didn't feel sad anymore. In fact, I was so busy trying to decide what to wear the next day that I didn't even notice how subdued my daughter had suddenly become.

Chapter Five

I'd never been to the Melrose Inn but I'd heard it was a pretty fancy place. In Natchez that meant you should wear what you'd wear to church—if you went to church, and I usually didn't. The sparseness of my wardrobe, not to mention the cold feet I kept getting, told me that I really had become almost a recluse in the past couple of years. I finally chose a coral outfit whose color was good on me although the style was out-of-date. As I drove to the inn I was far from satisfied with how I looked.

I reminded myself that this was probably a kind of business meeting, not a date. Len Percy didn't seem like the kind of a man who would pay much attention to clothes, anyway. Nevertheless, I felt a little nervous as I pulled through the inn's semicircular driveway to the parking lot in the rear.

The Melrose Inn is really a hotel-motel place that just happens to have a good restaurant. It's new, which is to say built sometime in the present century, of red brick with white trim. Not particularly distinguished architecturally, but attractive. The heat coming off the asphalt of the parking lot was like stepping into a blast furnace when I got out of my car's air-conditioning.

Len was waiting in the lobby. He looked cool and neat in a seersucker jacket over tan trousers. I felt as if I'd half melted just walking from the parking lot— it had to be over a hundred degrees out there.

"Hi," he said, "glad you could make it."

"So am I." He stood back and let me precede him into the restaurant. I was terribly self-conscious, sure that perspiration was dripping down my neck in a most unfeminine way. I had done my hair up on top of my head in a kind of Victorian pouf, and I was afraid the high humidity had turned all my artfully escaping little tendrils into rat tails. Oh, well.

The brunch was buffet-style. As we served ourselves I remarked, "Except that there's more food here, this reminds me of eating at Cottonwood Hall."

"Um-hmm," he agreed, "I wish I had an excuse to be there at mealtime every day."

When we'd sat down again at our table I looked at our plates and commented, "For a doctor and a nurse, you and I don't make a very good advertisement for healthy eating." We both had bacon and sausage and biscuits and scrambled eggs and cheese grits in front of us.

Len grinned. "I always figure eating out is the time to forget all that stuff. I watch my cholesterol level in secret."

I confessed, "I don't watch mine at all."

For a while we simply ate. I couldn't tell if Len found it hard to make conversation, or if he was just hungry. I began to feel uncomfortable with the silence, so I asked where he'd gone to medical school.

"Tulane. Did my residency in Jackson."

"How did you end up in Natchez?"

"I wanted to be in a small town, didn't want to stay in Jackson. Did want to stay in Mississippi because my family's here, my parents are getting old and I felt like I should be around. They live in Hattiesburg."

"Somehow I don't think of Natchez as a small town."

"It is, though. In fact, I'm wondering if there are enough people here to support a psychiatrist. One of the reasons I chose Natchez was that there was no psychiatrist in private practice here—now I begin to understand why. Getting my practice off the ground is a struggle."

"What about the man who was at Cottonwood Hall before you, what's his name, Stewart? He didn't have his own practice?"

"Not in Natchez. He lives in Vidalia, drove across the bridge to get to the Hall. I don't want to live or work in Arkansas, even if it is just across the River. What about you, how'd you get here?"

"Sometimes I wonder about that myself. I just kind of ended up here. I was looking for a place to settle and have my baby—the little girl I told you about—and when I got to Natchez I liked it, thought the town had a nice atmosphere. So I decided to stay. Of course it was springtime then, I hadn't had a taste of the summer heat!"

"You're not originally from around here?"

"No. I grew up in Tennessee, in the mountains not far from Nashville. It can get warm in the mountains, but not like this."

"Um." Len was an attentive audience. "And then? I mean, after you grew up in the Tennessee mountains?"

I couldn't look at him. I looked down at my plate, carefully cutting a piece of sausage into unnecessarily tiny bits. "I left home. Against my parents' wishes." It had been a selfish decision. I knew that. I still felt guilty about it. Probably I always would.

Len waited. I knew he was eating but he was also watching me, I could feel it. Well, I was the one who had started with the personal questions. I might as well go on. "I volunteered for the Army as soon as I was old enough—at eighteen, as soon as I graduated from high school. I stayed in the Army until after my husband was killed. He was a helicopter pilot and he was on a routine flight—it was an accident."

"I'm sorry. I didn't mean for you to have to get into that." His voice was gentle.

Now I looked up, into kind eyes that were brown, a lighter brown than mine. "It's okay. It happened five years ago. I'm mostly over it now. Anyway, that's how I got to Natchez. They were sympathetic about me not wanting to stay in the Army after that, let me resign. I was newly pregnant, tried going home to Tennessee but that didn't work out—and here I am!"

"Well, I for one am very glad you're here." Len's smile was different from his perpetual grin—it was tender, as much a smile of the eyes as the lips.

When I smiled back at him and said, "So am I," I felt something let go, dissolve inside me, as if for years I'd carried a lump of ice around my heart and now it was gone.

A waiter came to the table and refilled our coffee cups. When he'd left I said, "What was it that you wanted to talk to me about?"

"Huh?" He raised his eyebrows, and then he did the most remarkable thing—he blushed. His face didn't exactly turn red because he had a tan, but his tan deepened.

His embarrassment touched me. I understood now why he'd encouraged me to talk about myself: he'd really wanted to know. This wasn't a business meeting after all, and my heart sang with gladness.

I decided to rescue Len out of his discomfort. "When you called and said you wanted to talk to me, I was hoping it had something to do with Cottonwood Hall. I thought I'd like to talk to you, too. How is Belinda Stokes? Do you know any more about what happened to her?"

He shook his head. "No. She's got me stumped. Her lithium level was okay, so it wasn't that. Electrolyte balance was okay. Everything I could think of and the internal medicine doc on the hospital staff could think of checked out, but there she is, still comatose. The nurses reported a couple of times that they thought she was coming out of it, and once when I examined her I thought so myself. But she didn't. She hasn't." He clutched his head as if that would help him to think, and messed up his hair. "I don't

know.... Her heart is strong. I expect she'll make it.
I guess we'll never know what the hell happened."

I remembered that awful scream—I'd never forget
it. "I read everything in her chart—I'm sure you did,
too—and it does say that she'd been hallucinating before the day she collapsed. The night nurse reported
it."

"Um-hmm. That's another thing—unless she really was seeing Lilibet's ghost, there's no reason for
her to have had hallucinations. As I said, her lithium
level was where it should have been. Doc Stewart had
a lot of trouble getting her stabilized, but he'd done it.
And then this happens. Anyway, Amanda, I didn't ask
you out to talk about Belinda Stokes. I guess maybe
you figured out by now, I just wanted to be with you.
Start getting to know you."

"That's nice," I said, and my heart began to beat
too fast. So I rushed on, "But I did want to talk to you
about work, too. Let's get some dessert, so the waiter
will stop eyeing our table like a buzzard about to
swoop, and talk a little longer."

For a while the pastry cart had all our attention. I
chose a layered flaky thing that I guessed was a Na-
poleon—I'm not all that familiar with fancy past-
ries—and Len took cheesecake with raspberry de-
signs on top.

Finally I put down my fork and said, "There's
something that bothers me about Cottonwood Hall. I
realize I've only been on the job there for two days,
but still ... Len, why is there no psychotherapy? No
recreation program? No occupational therapy?"
These were all features of what I'd been taught was a

well-rounded approach to caring for mental patients and getting them ready to go back into the world again.

"Cottonwood Hall is a different kind of facility, Amanda. As Doc Stewart explained it to me, the goal there is to maintain the patients—excuse me, residents, Stark would have my head—maintain them as comfortably as possible."

"Which is done purely on drug therapy."

"Correct."

"Don't I know it! As the RN, I spend most of my time giving meds, recording meds, taking vital signs to monitor meds, counting meds at the end of the shift. Len, those folks are all on high doses of their drugs. All except Miss Lilibet."

"That's because there is no drug specific to Alzheimer's Disease. As the disease progresses she'll develop some agitation, and when that happens I'll have to start her on Haldol."

"Still, with the others, it's as if somebody—I guess your predecessor Dr. Stewart—had determined their drug levels backwards from the way I was taught."

"I don't quite follow you." Len wasn't liking this, I could tell by the way he'd begun to shift in his chair and look anywhere but at me.

"The way I was taught is to determine the smallest possible amount of tranquilizer, antidepressant, whatever, that will counteract the abnormality. At Cottonwood Hall, it seems like the patients, *residents,* are all given the highest doses they can possibly tolerate without side effects. It's like, zap 'em with the psychotropics as hard as you can, and don't let up until you have to!" I was incensed, I'd raised my voice without realizing it.

Len leaned across the table. "Shh. The walls might have ears, Amanda."

Now it was my turn to blush. "Sorry."

The stern note in his voice sounded forced. "It's the psychiatrist's job, not the nurse's, to determine the proper medication, and the level of medication. You know that."

"Of course I do. And you're the psychiatrist." I tried another approach. "As a psychiatrist, surely the complete absence of psychotherapy must bother you?"

He relented a little. "You don't seem to understand what I said before. The goal is to maintain the residents, not to return them to the community. These folks aren't going anywhere. Either they don't have homes to go back to, like Miss Lilibet whose house has been sold, or their families don't want them back. What would be the point of psychotherapy?"

I pushed a few flaky pastry bits around on my plate. "They might not get completely well, but they could get better. I just hate to see people drugged to their eyeballs all day long, that's all."

"Come on," Len said decisively. "Let's get out of here. There's something more I want to say to you, but I'd rather do it where we can have some privacy."

We went for a drive in his car, an extremely beat-up old Chevy, so that we could have both privacy and air-conditioning. Len looked grim. I kept quiet and waited for him to speak. When he did, what he said surprised me.

"I wondered about it, too. I asked Doc Stewart some of the same things you've just asked me. You're a sharp woman, Amanda, and obviously a good nurse. Even if you've been away from it for a while."

"I didn't tell you that."

He grinned and hunched his shoulders. "I read your résumé, that's where I got your address and phone number. Staff doc has legitimate access to personnel records."

"That's no problem, Len. But the other is. I'm sorry, but it still bothers me. It doesn't make sense, in a place where money is obviously not an issue, for there to be insufficient staff and a poor treatment program."

"Okay, I'll give it to you straight. You're right, there's not enough staff to do any extras. But the people are comfortable." He took his eyes from the road for a moment and shot me a piercing look. "You ever see a place in your life any more comfortable than Cottonwood Hall?"

"I guess not. But here's a question for you. Is there a difference between comfortableness, and quality of life? I think there is. I think you have to have some quality of life before you even really care if you're *comfortable,* or not. If I was zonked out on zillions of milligrams of tranquillizers, like some I could mention, where's my quality of life? So I get to eat off china plates and out of silver serving dishes—does that really make me *comfortable?*"

Len pounded the steering wheel with one hand, and I saw that his gentle nature had limits. I was making him angry. Good!

"You're splitting hairs, Amanda. You're also talking to a guy who's done his turn at the state mental hospital, and treated the homeless mentally ill in the emergency room in Jackson. Hell, I've even gone out on the street and tried to treat them there. Pardon me if I don't get all uptight trying to distinguish quality of life from comfortableness when it comes to the residents of Cottonwood Hall!''

"Okay. Sorry, I guess I got a little carried away."

"Yeah. You're forgiven."

We were silent. Eventually, carefully, I said, "So what we're doing at Cottonwood Hall, really, is warehousing the rich?"

"That's essentially it, Amanda. Yes. And I don't intend to make waves. I need that job. I'm fresh out of residency and med school, and I'm getting a late start. I'm thirty-five, and I've got loans to pay off out the wazoo. It'll be a good five, six years before I start to make any money for *me* instead of to pay back the banks, and in the meantime I'm poor as a church mouse. So you can believe I won't make waves! I need this job. And if you need your job, I suggest you don't make any, either."

"I do need it," I murmured. I hadn't realized what his situation was, and I felt a tad ashamed that I'd provoked him into revealing it.

Len turned the car around and drove back to the Melrose Inn. All the way back I rationalized. There was certainly nothing criminal going on at Cottonwood Hall, no insurance fraud if all the residents were paying their own way. All of the staff—even Sally, in her own flighty way—seemed to be genuinely concerned about the residents. Furthermore, the residents were being maintained in a style to which they were accustomed. The sound of Len's voice interrupted my thoughts.

"You've been mighty quiet." He pulled to a stop in the parking lot behind my car.

"I know. I'm sorry. I didn't mean anything I said to be a criticism of you, Len. I hope you understand that."

He held out his hand. "Friends?"

I placed my hand in his. "Friends." He pulled me toward him and kissed me. It was a light kiss that soon deepened in a way that promised more than simple friendship.

LEN'S KISS, so pleasant while it lasted, threw me into a turmoil as soon as he drove away. I felt as if I were coming unglued. I knew this was irrational, I hated it, but I couldn't help it, either. I couldn't go home to little Sam in such a state, and I'd said I'd be home by three and it was almost three—damn! Well, I'd just have to be a little late.

I drove to a place on the bluff where you can see the river. I'd gone there before when I needed to sort things out. There's something about a large body of water that calms me, helps me put everything into perspective. So I looked at the wide Mississippi on its eternal roll toward the sea, and I thought about Sam. Not little Sam, big Sam. Sam Matthews, my dead husband.

I cried for a while, quietly, big silent tears welling in my eyes and rolling down my cheeks. Rolling, as the river rolls.

I remembered the feel of Len's mouth on mine…and the desire he had stirred in me. Hot, deep, disturbing desire. In all my life before today I'd felt such desire for only one man—Sam Matthews.

I'd loved Sam so much, so very, very much. And he'd loved me—oh, how he'd loved me! Coming as I did from a family so strict, so austere that physical expressions of affection were frowned upon even between parent and child, I hadn't known until Sam how it felt to be loved. To love and be loved, to touch, to kiss, together to make a child. Oh!

My tears rolled down.

And then to lose him without warning. To have the cherished new life—a new life half his—growing within my very body, and then to lose him… The pain of loss was so great it had been like a physical weight, a crushing, crushing thing. In that agony to go home—*home is where when you go there, they have to take you in*—and find I no longer had a home, they would not take me in. No home. No love. All gone, the love.

That was when I'd found where the love still lived, still thrived: in my mind, in my heart, in my soul. Then, when she was born the love lived in little Sam, too. Our child of my body. She multiplied the love, our love—big Sam's and mine—and that love was as necessary to me as breathing. Without it, without the love still alive in me for my dead husband, I didn't know how to exist.

So I was in a turmoil, because for the first time since Sam's death, I had met a man who awakened my desire. Not like the others I'd known from time to time and dismissed without a qualm. Len was different. Simply being with him had melted a lump of ice I hadn't even known I carried within me until I felt it leave. I knew, I could tell without reason or question, that I could grow to love Len Percy. If he loved me. If I allowed myself to love him.

My tears had stopped. The turmoil was over. And the river rolled on.

SAMANTHA WAS in the yard all by herself when I drove up. She didn't come running, she just stood and waited until I came to her and put my arms around her. It wasn't like my little girl to be so quiet.

"Where's Sally, honey?"

"She's in the house. Watching television. Maybe she's talking on the telephone. You were gone an awful long time, Mommy. I was worried."

"It's just three-thirty, honey. I'm a little late, that's all."

"But you're never late!"

"Well sweetie, then this is the first time and there will probably be other times. Sometimes you just can't help it." I took her hand and began to walk toward the back door. To my surprise she hung back.

"Why can't you help it?" This was not a straight-forward question, she said it in a whining tone. If I'd never been late before, then Sam certainly had never sounded like this before. She sounded spoiled, and I didn't like that one bit.

I sat on the back steps so that I was on her level and put my hands on her shoulders. "Sam, sometimes things happen and you get delayed. You know I'll always come back. When I take you to school, I always come and pick you up, and when I go out and leave you with a sitter, I always come back. There's nothing to worry about, is there?"

"N-no." But she didn't sound convinced.

"Tell you what, I'll promise you something, and then I want you to promise me something. I promise that if I'm ever going to be really, really late I'll call and let you know. Half an hour isn't really late, but if it's going to be as much as an hour I'll call. Okay? You've been learning to tell time, you know how long that is, don't you?"

Sam nodded. Her eyes were round and wide.

"Now you promise me that you'll try to understand if I'm a little late once in a while. Okay?"

"Okay. I promise." Now she smiled, and her little arms came around my neck in a great big hug. "I love you, Mommy."

"I love you too, Sam." That was a relief!

We went inside and I tried to pay Sally, but she wouldn't hear of it. She said instead that she'd been glad to stay with Sam and she hoped I'd ask her again. How nice, I thought.

But later that night after I'd put Sam to bed, she got up and came padding in her bare feet out to the living room where I sat reading a book.

"Mommy, I gots to tell you something."

"It must be important. I thought you were asleep."

She nodded solemnly. She looked like a dark-eyed little angel, with her auburn hair mussed and fanned out around her head. She said, "I don't like Sally."

"Why, Sam! We've known Sally for ages, she's our neighbor, and you never said such a thing before."

"She didn't never baby-sit me before."

"Did she do anything, or say anything, to make you not like her?"

I could see the wheels of thought turning, with difficulty, in my daughter's eyes. Finally she said, "Not zackly. She just makes me uncunsterble."

"You mean uncomfortable. Do you really know what that word means, honey?"

"Uncunsterble means like when you have to go to the bathroom and you're in the car so you have to wait."

That was as good a definition as I'd ever heard, whether she could pronounce the word yet or not. "Okay, I understand. Sally makes you feel uncomfortable. But what does she *do* that makes you feel that way?"

"I don't know, that's just how I feel when she's close up. That's why I went out in the yard to wait for you. She didn't care, she doesn't like me anyway, I can tell. Mommy, I don't mind if you have to go places and I have to have a sitter, and I really, really will keep the promise about if you're late, but please, please don't get Sally to stay with me again. Please?"

Even for a mature four-year-old, that was quite a speech. "If you feel that strongly about it, Sam, of course I won't. I promise. Now come on, let's get you back to bed."

When I'd tucked her in and kissed her cheek and gotten a damp smack on my cheek in return, my daughter had one last surprise for me. "Mommy, I think I don't want to be called Sam anymore. I want to be called Samantha. That's my real name, isn't it?"

"Of course it is, you know that. But I've always called you Sam. Why would you rather be called Samantha all of a sudden?"

"Because I have to go to school again tomorrow, with all those new kids, and they make fun of me. They say that Sam's a boy's name and I'm a girl. Besides, I like Samantha. It's a pretty name, it sounds nicer."

"Well, it's your name and if that's what you want, that's what you shall have, Samantha."

"Good." She snuggled down under the summer blanket. Already her eyes were heavy, closing. "Tell the teacher, too. Tell her my name's really Samantha." And with that she was gone, into the instant, deep sleep of childhood.

"I'll tell her, Samantha," I whispered.

I thought, as I cracked the door, that I didn't have to call her Sam in order to keep her father's memory alive. I would always see him in the lines of her face, in the color of her hair, every day of her life. Samantha, indeed.

This had been quite a day.

Chapter Six

We had too many storms that summer. Too many, too violent. I knew that most people welcomed them, so I was ashamed to admit they scared me. Most Mississippians were like Miss Lilibet—they had childhood memories of summers before houses were air-conditioned, when they would sit on their porches and wait for a thunderstorm to break the heat. I had no such memories, and all that clashing and booming and strangeness of light nearly broke *me*.

The storms were too many, too violent, and too often they came while I was working at Cottonwood Hall. I think I could have continued to bear up under the strain if I'd been at home with Sam. She, who was sticking to her wish to be called Samantha, could be numbered among those born and bred in Mississippi. Maybe it was something they put in the water, I didn't know, but thunderstorms didn't scare Samantha one bit. I'd taught her all the safety rules about lightning, I'd told her that thunder was only the sound of clouds bumping their heads together, and I was used to hiding my own unreasoning fear when I was with her, for her sake. But when I was working at Cottonwood Hall I didn't have to put on a brave face for my daughter, and unreasoning fear held full sway.

In the week following that significant Sunday we had three storms and each was worse than the one before it. On that Monday Belinda Stokes died in the hospital, and of all the ridiculous, primitive things I'd ever heard of, her body was brought back to Cottonwood Hall to lie in state in an open coffin in the parlor. And as if that were not enough, two patients started going downhill—*decompensating* is the technical term.

Both the patients who got into trouble were male, one an elderly ninety-two and the other quite young, in his twenties. The old man had a diagnosis of senile dementia; the young one was autistic. The old man, Magnus Everett, was a sweetheart of an old southern gentleman and already a favorite of mine. His room was in the main house, at the end of the hallway opposite the now empty room of Belinda Stokes. The young man, Tom Parker, I knew scarcely at all—his room was in the new wing and because of his autism he was resistant even to the taking of vital signs.

It was during the second thunderstorm that I first noticed Magnus was not his usual self. I was not my usual self either, because of the storm, but that was beside the point. Remembering my first day when all the electricity had failed, I'd armed myself with a heavy-duty flashlight. I stood in front of the French doors that opened onto the porch on the second floor, and from there I kept watch over the residents. I'd told them to stay in their rooms until the storm passed.

The electricity had not gone out but I was afraid that it would. The lights kept dimming and flickering and would occasionally wink off and then wink back on again. I'd sent Jones to monitor the residents in the new wing, and to tell them to stay in their rooms, with the exception of Miss Lilibet. If she wanted to wander it was fine with me. She gathered a lot of interesting information in her wandering. I was already, without realizing it, beginning to think of Lilibet as my personal spy.

There was a lull in the thunder and lightning. The house seemed to sigh, but remained watchful. I knew we were in for a second assault, I could feel that premonitory heaviness in the air even through the closed windows and through the closed doors at my back. The lights flickered—another warning. Outside I heard an ominous murmur from the cottonwood trees.

I thought about the body of Belinda Stokes lying in deceptive peacefulness inside her dark mahogany coffin upon a bier draped in black, candles burning at her head and feet. It was in her will, they said, that she should lie this way for three days, then she was to be cremated and her ashes scattered over the river. The cottonwoods shrieked, the lights dimmed and stayed at half-mast. I wondered if Miss Lilibet was in the parlor with Belinda, waiting to see if the ghost of Cottonwood Hall might pay a visit to the coffin during this storm.

Now again the thunder rolled—long, low, threatening, gathering itself up. The eerie yellow-green light of the storm seeped its way along the walls. I was all tension, all nerves; I wanted to tear down the stairs and run across the lawn and lose myself among the cottonwood trees, shrieking along with them. I could well understand why Lilibet believed ghosts walked in weather such as this.

A silent sheet of lightning lit the hallway like a merciless strobe. Another, and another. The thunder rumbled, moving, lumbering. Suddenly—with a great *Crack!*—the storm began again. The sound was deafening, maddening, wave after wave so vast that the walls and the floor shook. And in the midst of all this came ancient Magnus staggering from his room.

I knew it was Magnus, but for uncounted moments I stood with my heart in my throat, because the creature who clawed his way up the hall did not look like the Magnus I knew. The Magnus Everett I knew had Jones dress him each day in the height of style for a gentleman-planter of about sixty years ago: creamy white suit, brocaded silk tie, golden watch chain draped across his vest. He always wore a broad-brimmed white hat although he remained indoors, and he always had in hand an ebony walking stick with a gold knob on top although he seldom walked any farther than a chair in the hall. There, or in his room, he would sit and nod and smile to himself, talking in a soft voice of many things—all of them totally unrelated to the reality around him. Sometimes silently he would cry, but his tears were like a gentle shower, soon replaced by the sun of his sweet smile.

What I saw now, I did not want to believe. Magnus was a horrible, scrawny, naked apparition that gibbered as it came. The lights winked out. When they winked on again he was closer and I saw him claw the air with his left hand—and with his right, he brandished his ebony cane. Its heavy gold knob glinted as it slashed through the air. The lights went out, not a wink this time, and I did the only thing I could think of to do: I switched on my flashlight and swung the beam in Magnus's face, and blinded him.

The gibbering—I couldn't make out words, whatever he thought he was saying was full of gnashing sounds—became a roar and then a yelp and then a howl. The howl did not sound human, it sounded like the cry of a hopelessly cornered animal. A simultaneous crack of thunder and lightning swallowed it up. My flashlight was powerful, and Magnus was stunned by its pitiless beam. He threw his skinny arms up to protect his face, and dropped the cane. It clattered on the floor.

I called him by name. "Magnus! Magnus Everett!"

He grunted, still cowering in my light. The electricity hadn't come back on yet. How dangerous was he without the cane? I decided I didn't care. I walked toward him. He was about twelve feet from me, and I kept him pinned by my flashlight beam. I talked as I moved, hoping he could hear me over the now retreating thunder. I repeated his name often, to keep his attention, to try to bring him back—not to reality, he wasn't capable of that—but to some gentler state of delusion than whatever had caused this most fastidious of men to tear off all his clothes.

"It's all right now," I said as I reached him, "I'm here. I'm going to take care of you. You're safe now." I shielded the flashlight beam with my fingers, muting it, then kept it at waist level. "I'm Amanda, Magnus, you know me."

"Mandy?" He sounded querulous, hopeful. He'd called me Mandy from the first, but lost as he was in the past I knew that the name meant someone else to him, not me. I hadn't cared because whoever his Mandy was, he'd liked her and therefore he liked me.

"Yes, Mandy. I'm going to put my arm around you now. I'm going to help you. We're going home, Magnus." I wished with all my heart that the lights would come on again. They didn't.

"Bad, bad-bad-bad-bad," said Magnus. He was so thin that his age-slackened skin slid back and forth over bone where I grasped him. But he'd been a big man once, and even if he was all skin and bones now those bones were heavy. He gushed more gibberish and staggered, and for a moment I was afraid we would both fall under his weight.

"Magnus!" I said sharply, "we have to go home now!"

"Bad-bad. Shloshy lock ba-gok."

I kept putting one foot in front of the other and by sheer force of will got him to do the same. It was hard work. I couldn't do it and talk and hold the flashlight at the same time, so I said no more. Unfortunately his room was all the way at the opposite end of the hall.

Magnus continued to spout nonsense, but at least he wasn't violent. At one point he said something that sounded like "black riders."

Now that I felt we had things more or less under control, I was intensely curious. I wanted to know what he was seeing, hearing, what had upset him so much. But I wouldn't try to find out. My curiosity was of zero importance compared to the price this poor old man would have to pay if anything I did or said were to take him back into the horrible place he'd been.

So when I at last got Magnus into his room and onto his bed I said, "There. The bad is all gone now." He looked up at me in the pool of half-light from the shaded flash, and said quite clearly, "No, ma'am." There was a note of despair in his voice that chilled me, and tugged at my heart.

LEN CAME TO MY HOUSE that evening. I'd hated to leave Cottonwood Hall before he arrived to check on Magnus Everett, but I couldn't be late to pick up Samantha. So I'd left a note, asking him to call, and when he'd called I invited him over. He said he could be there at nine, he still had a couple of appointments back at his office.

Samantha was already in bed and asleep when Len arrived. I'd made a pot of decaffeinated coffee. When I asked if he'd eaten he admitted he hadn't, so I gave him two meat loaf sandwiches. He ate like a starved teenager. It was ridiculous, I knew, but I got a kind of secret female pleasure watching him devour food I'd prepared.

"How is Magnus?" I asked as Len started on his second sandwich.

"Resting quietly. When I got there the evening shift nurse had given him the Restoril prescribed for sleep. I couldn't do much of an examination, but I read your notes in the chart. Your notes are good, Amanda, very thorough. Much better than the other nurses'."

"Thank you. But I wish she hadn't given Magnus sleeping meds before you had a chance to examine him. I mean, certainly nobody wanted him to turn psychotic again, but I think he'd have been okay until you arrived if she'd just stayed with him. Sally offered, but Sally has no training so I told her no."

My hair was down, the way I usually wear it around the house, and now I pulled a strand of it over my shoulder and twisted it around and around my finger—an old habit when something's worrying me. "That's just another example of not having enough staff! We should at the very least have two nursing assistants. And while I'm complaining, I might as well add that the nursing assistants we do have should be better trained than they are. Ephraim Jones is a nice guy, he's inherently kind and he's more observant than most. He could be really good if he had specific training as a psychiatric aide. But Len, he's not even certified!"

Len shrugged, still working on the last of his sandwich. "Amanda, we went over this kind of thing the other day. As far as I know there's no violation, the state has no law about nursing assistants having to be certified."

I got up to get more coffee, not because we particularly needed a refill but because I was too agitated to sit still. From behind my back I heard Len say, "Uh—oh, nuts!"

I turned around. "Oh, nuts what?"

"I, uh, I wanted to pay you a compliment, and I'm just so lousy at things like that, I never know how to start. Anyway, you have the most beautiful hair,

Amanda. I wondered how long it was, how it would look if you didn't have it up or back the way you usually wear it. And it, it's just plain beautiful.''

My hair is waist-length and straight as a stick, totally unfashionable. But I've kept it that way because Sam Matthews had liked my long, straight hair. Now I smiled for Len, who liked it, too. "You said that very nicely. I don't think you were lousy at it." His plate was empty. "Would you like some dessert to go with your coffee? I can offer cherry pie or chocolate chip cookies, courtesy of my daughter who chooses the sweets around here. Within certain limits, of course."

"Yes thanks, cherry pie. Where is your daughter?"

"She's asleep. Being in daycare—she calls it school—full-time tires her out better than anything I've been able to think of since she was born! She sacks out at eight o'clock these days. Here you go. It's Mrs. Smith's pie, not Amanda Matthews's, but it's still pretty good."

"Mmm. Sure is."

A part of me wanted to forget why I'd asked Len to come over, wanted to do no more than rediscover the succession of little joys that come in getting to know someone you're sure you will like very much. But the other part of me won out, the part that had a genuine concern but could also hide behind professionalism whenever I got cold feet. I made a leading statement. "I suppose we'll never know what it was that happened to Magnus Everett this afternoon."

"Your chart notes said he'd had a psychotic episode. I changed his medication based on your judgment, and now you tell me we don't *know* what happened this afternoon?" Len's sandy hair fell over his forehead, there were lines of tiredness under his eyes. He looked as if he simply could not handle one more thing today, and I felt guilty. But not guilty enough to give up.

"What I meant was, since Magnus's senility is usually so mild-natured, and since he was already on a fairly high regular dose of a mild tranquilizer, I wonder what happened to change him from mild to violent? Len, haven't you noticed that there isn't much information in any of our patients' charts? Just the current year's notes and a brief medical history."

Len pushed the hair back off his forehead and tipped his chair back. "The notes from previous years, and a full history, are kept in the administrator's office, under lock and key, not to mention the baleful eye of Frances Stark. I know because I had to get Belinda Stokes' complete records from her after Stokes was admitted to the hospital. You could brave the baleful eye and request Everett's records if you think you really need them, but I doubt they'll tell you anything. The man's mind is gone, Amanda. He got worse today, it's that simple. You seem pretty determined to make something out of nothing."

"This is beginning to feel like Sunday afternoon all over again," I said unhappily. "The less pleasant part of Sunday afternoon, that is."

"Yeah." He paused, gazing abstractedly across the room. Then he righted his chair and leaned toward me. "But you know, Amanda, much as I hate to admit it, I'm getting concerned myself."

I wanted to say, *Finally!* but contented myself with raising my eyebrows.

Len continued, "I wanted to have an autopsy on Belinda Stokes, and I ran into a stone wall."

"I thought you said she developed pneumonia secondary to her coma. That's not so unusual, not truly an unexpected cause of death."

"Yeah. But it's kind of like you wanting to know why Everett all of a sudden had this uncharacteristic episode. I wanted to know why Stokes's pattern of behavior changed, why she had those hallucinations and then went into the coma in the first place, and why she never came out of it. Maybe an autopsy wouldn't have revealed anything, but I figured it was worth a shot."

"And you ran into a stone wall? That's odd, considering she doesn't seem to have had any next of kin."

"No next of kin, but she had a lawyer with full power of attorney, including a medical POA. And she had an airtight will with all sorts of provisions about how her body was to be handled when she died."

"That seems bizarre, doesn't it? Morbid. The residents go and look at her, you know. Miss Lilibet goes around with the soft voice of doom saying things like 'This could happen to any of us at any time.'" I shuddered. "It's horrible."

"All I know is her lawyer won't talk, says none of it's even open to discussion. No autopsy. The body is to lie in state at Cottonwood Hall for three days and then be cremated, and the ashes scattered—by him—in the Mississippi River. End of discussion."

We were both silent for a while. Gloomy.

At last I put my thoughts into words. "I wonder what Belinda's will says about the inheritance. Who gets her money?"

I HAD TO GIVE Sally credit—she was hanging in there. Tom Parker, autistic and twenty-two, sat cross-legged on the floor of his room, rocking back and forth. On every forward motion he bashed his head into the foot of his bed as hard as he could. It made a sickening sound. The bedstead was brass with decorative curlicues and on these, Tom had injured himself. Oblivious to his own blood, Tom continued. Rock, bam! Rock, bam! Rock, bam! From his throat came a hollow, monotonous, nasal tone like the droning of a bagpipe.

Sally had paged me on the intercom, but for several seconds she didn't notice that I'd arrived. I made a swift assessment of the situation, then looked over at Sally—and faltered. The expression of rapt fascination on her face was to me almost as horrible as Tom Parker's head bashing.

But I had no time to think about this. I snapped, "Sally, go get Jones. Tell him we'll need restraints. And close the door behind you. There's no need for the other patients to be gawking at Tom." I knew I should have said "residents," but I was past caring.

Sally gulped, "Yes, Amanda!" I'd startled her; she'd practically been in a trance. *Entranced*, I thought, wrinkling my nose in distaste, but I soon forgot all about Sally.

Autistic people are not intentionally violent either to themselves or others. However, they seem to have no concept of physical pain and therefore pain—their own or someone else's—is no deterrent for them. They are completely single-minded, and this gives them the appearance of being unusually strong-willed. When they are distressed, autistic people frequently seem to get relief from repetitive motions, especially rocking. I knew all this and more, but it didn't help much with Tom Parker.

He wouldn't stop rocking. He wouldn't stop banging his head. He didn't respond to anything Jones or I said. In fact, I doubted he heard even the droning sound that he himself continued to make.

"Have you ever seen him like this before?" I asked Jones in a low voice.

"No, Miss Amanda, I haven't seen *anything* like this before," said Jones.

No training, I thought bitterly. I hated to put anyone in restraints, so I knelt next to Tom and tried once more to stop his rocking. It was no use; the young man's body, all muscles tensed, was as resistant as solid metal and I was no match for him. I told Jones what to do and thanked God for his superior strength while he did it.

Jones's pleasant, youthful face was creased with compassion. "You sure you don't want to give him something? Maybe he'll sleep, forget. Be better when he wakes up."

"No. That's for Dr. Percy to decide. Go and call the doctor, please, and I'll stay here until he comes."

Once Jones had picked up Tom bodily from the floor and worked his resistant arms into the restraint

vest, we'd put him into his rocking chair and tied the
long straps of the vest to the spindles of the chair back.

"That's a much better way to rock, isn't it," I said,
even though I doubted he could hear me. I continued
to make soothing sounds as I bathed his bobbing head
with a soapy washcloth while he rocked back and
forth, back and forth. The head injury was superfi-
cial, nothing serious, but it had bled a lot. Tom had
stopped the droning noise when Jones picked him up,
but as he rocked he'd started it again. Perhaps in his
mind it was a sound that went with rocking; perhaps,
in his bleak autistic world, a mother's lullaby sounded
like that to him. So sad.

Once I'd put a butterfly bandage on Tom's forehead cut, there was nothing more I could do. I stopped
trying to talk to him, because his droning was drown-
ing me out. On a good day Tom Parker was capable of
following simple directions, though he was nowhere
near as adapted to the world as the Dustin Hoffman
character had been in *Rain Man*—the only example of
adult autism most people were familiar with. I knew
there was no point in telling Tom not to rock so hard,
so I didn't even try. I did try not to let the droning
noise bother me—but it was near the end of my shift
and near the end of the week, and I was tired and my
nerves were shot.

At least there had been no storm this afternoon. Not
so far, anyway. I glanced out of the window—outside
everything was pale gray and still. All day the skies had
been obscured by high, dull clouds, the air so heavy
and humid it lay over Natchez like a cloying blanket.

Fitting weather for scattering ashes: they had taken Belinda Stokes to be cremated this morning.

"What happened here?"

I must have jumped a foot. "Frances!" I hadn't heard her open the door, but there stood the administrator of Cottonwood Hall in her usual dark-suited severity.

"Well?" she demanded.

Tom Parker rocked harder. Whether he did this in response to some cue within his own isolated brain, or at some level he was aware of a change in the room, there was no way to know. All I knew was that if he rocked any harder than this he might turn the chair over. I couldn't leave him, and I wasn't going to talk about him in his presence, either. I said, "I'll explain after Dr. Percy gets here. I sent Jones to call him."

"I know that," said Frances Stark, striding into the middle of the room. Her eyes narrowed as she studied the patient—surely even she would not call Tom a resident at this point—and she pressed her lips together in a grim line. She didn't like this. I wondered if she didn't like it because she hated to see Tom Parker suffer, or because it represented another hitch in the running of her institution.

Tom Parker rocked furiously. I moved behind the rocking chair so that I could hold on to its back, perhaps slow him down a little.

Frances shifted her gaze to me. She looked at me so hard and so long that I felt like a butterfly impaled on a pin. Finally she said, "You know, Matthews, if I hadn't seen with my own eyes how you handled Belinda Stokes that day, I'd be wondering about you."

My throat went dry. "I ... I don't understand what you mean."

"I mean since you came here, seems like all hell has started breaking loose."

"If you'll remember, hell started breaking loose *before* you hired me."

"Must have been right about the time you first put your foot in the door."

I remembered. Cold fear sliced into me. What would I do if I lost this job, my first in so many years? "Coincidence," I said shakily. "Surely, Mrs. Stark, you can't think I'm responsible for Stokes or Everett or—" I made an exaggerated nod at Tom Parker. I would not say his name, nor under any circumstances break my own rule.

She looked from me to him and back to me. The stern lines of her face softened somewhat. Or was that wishful thinking on my part? She said, "I thought I told you to call me Frances."

I felt a rush of gratitude that I knew was ridiculously out of proportion. I desperately wanted to talk to her. At the same time, my arm was beginning to ache from holding so tightly to the back of the rocking chair and I knew I couldn't leave. "Frances, as soon as Dr. Percy gets here I'll come to your office and we can talk. I just can't do it here."

"Never mind. But I strongly suggest you sedate this young man and put him to bed, for his own sake. Young Percy isn't coming. I hear he's got problems of his own."

Chapter Seven

I sat on the couch next to Sam. Excuse me. Samantha. Big Bird was explaining that this program was brought to us by the letter *P* and the number 4, and Samantha was making little puffing noises—"Puh, puh, puh"—the sound of the letter *P*. She was learning the sounds of the letters in school. Between that and "Sesame Street" I figured she'd be reading in no time.

I leaned my head back and said to her, "Wake me up for Cookie Monster." Cookie Monster is my favorite.

The phone rang and Samantha scrambled up to answer it. Not even "Sesame Street" can keep my daughter from the delight of answering the telephone. I heard her say in her most grown-up voice, "Hello. Can I help you?"

Then silence. Without moving I opened my eyes, expecting her to stretch out her little arm with the receiver in hand and say, "It's for you, Mommy." She didn't.

I closed my eyes again. Samantha had her own friends and they were now old enough that sometimes they called each other with some sort of invitation.

I smiled at the gravelly voice of Oscar the Grouch, who was counting on TV. Even with my eyes closed I could see him throwing things—one, two, three, four—out of his trash can. I was so tired, I felt as if I could sleep in a trash can myself.

"I think it was a wrong number," said Samantha a minute later as she settled next to me again, "because whoever it was didn't say anything."

"Mmm," I agreed, thinking nothing of it.

I didn't wake up for Cookie Monster, I woke up to a Four-Eyed, Four-Horned Flying Purple People Eater. Who else would be guest star of a program that is brought to you by the letter *P* and the Number 4?

THE TELEPHONE didn't ring again until 9:30 that night. I'd just gotten out of the shower, so I clutched the towel around my still wet body and hurried to pick up in my bedroom. My heart gave a little leap, even as I shoved down the hope. I hadn't heard from Len in over a week.

"Hello?"

Nothing. Silence.

"Hello," I said again. Wet in an air-conditioned room, I shivered. I still heard nothing. I said, "I think we have a bad connection. I'm going to hang up," and did. Then I remembered that Sam had answered the phone earlier and said it was a wrong number, nobody was there. Maybe the phone was out of order. I picked up the receiver and heard a dial tone—it sounded all right to me. I hung up again, feeling a little puzzled.

I had put on my robe and was combing out my hair when the phone rang again. I crossed the room and picked it up.

"Hello?"

This time I heard someone breathing. I said, "I can hear you. Can you hear me?" I was thinking that I might have a problem of the sort where I could call out but when people called in the connection was poor on their end.

The breathing sound got louder, as if someone were deliberately panting into the telephone.

The chill I felt this time did not come from air-conditioning. Nevertheless I said firmly, "This is ridiculous!" and I slammed down the phone. I went back to combing and then brushing my damp hair until it was dry. This is an activity that I find either tedious or soothing, depending on how much of a hurry I'm in. Tonight I was in no hurry but I didn't feel soothed, either. Trite or not, that panting on the telephone had sounded obscene, and I was shaken. All the more so when I thought about my number being unlisted.

The telephone rang again. My heart went up into my throat. I looked at the clock: ten minutes to ten. The phone continued to ring: one, two, three, four times. Just like on "Sesame Street," I thought. My heart immediately dropped back down where it belonged and I leaped to pick up the phone.

"Hello!" I said savagely.

"Hi, uh . . . Amanda, is that you? This is Len."

The anger flooded out of me like air from a pricked balloon. "Oh, Len!" I sank down on the bed. "I'm sorry, I thought you were a prank phone caller."

"I've tried a lot of odd things for kicks in my life, but never that. So far. What's up, Amanda? Somebody been bothering you?"

"Sort of. Nothing very original, just your standard heavy breathing obscene phone-caller type of stuff."

"How long has this been going on?"

"Just tonight. I'm sure it's nothing, it won't happen again. Enough about me. It's nice to hear from you." As soon as the words were out of my mouth I could have kicked myself. I was supposed to be mad at this man or at least disappointed in him. Not only hadn't I seen or heard from him for almost two weeks, but he'd done absolutely nothing for either of the patients I was so worried about.

"Likewise. I, uh, I've had a few problems lately. That's why I didn't call or anything. I'd been hoping we could get together again over the weekend last week, but..."

His voice trailed off and I let it, I nearly had to bite my tongue in half, but I didn't jump in to help.

Len seemed to get a second wind. "Well, I think I've got everything in hand as much as I can for now, so I was wondering about Saturday."

"The day after tomorrow," I said, as much to myself as to him. Dimly from someplace like adolescence I remembered something about not being too available.

"Yeah. I was thinking, if you're free maybe you and your daughter would like to spend part of the day with me."

"Well—"

"What I had in mind was, I live in an apartment—it isn't much but we do have a pretty nice swimming pool and I thought maybe your daughter might enjoy it. And afterwards I could cook out. I have a patio, it's about the size of a postage stamp but I can do a pretty good steak out there…unless Samantha would rather have hot dogs. I could do hot dogs for her and steaks for us. How about it, Amanda?"

I tossed all the lessons of my adolescence to the wind—that hadn't been my favorite time of life anyway. "I'd love it, and I'm sure Samantha would, too. On one condition—you let me bring a salad, or something."

"Salad." A yearning note came into Len's voice. "You wouldn't by any chance consider making potato salad, would you?"

I grinned. "I make the meanest potato salad south of Memphis. I'll be glad to bring it."

"That's great!"

We agreed on a time and I wrote down the directions to his apartment. Sam was going to be out of her mind with joy. She was always begging me to take her to the municipal pool and I was always putting her off because it was so crowded in the summer that I found it hard to keep an eye on her. I said as much to Len, and then I said goodbye.

"One more thing, Amanda," he said, drawing me back.

"Yes?"

"I was thinking about your obscene phone caller, and about your phone being unlisted."

"Um-hmm." Suddenly I was cold all over again.

"That makes it more serious."

"I suppose."

"Maybe you should report it to the police."

"If it happens again, maybe I will. But I don't think it will happen again."

THE NEXT DAY, Friday, I grabbed a fast salad for lunch. I intended to use most of my lunch hour checking out the exercise facilities Sally had told me were on the Hall's ground floor. Swimming pools meant bathing suits, and I was feeling out of shape. Half an hour on a stationary bike wouldn't really do much good, of course, but I'd feel virtuous. Such reasoning might not earn me an *A* in a college Logic course, but any woman would find it perfectly logical.

I hadn't the slightest idea how to get down there. When I thought about it, I didn't remember ever seeing a door that looked as if it might lead to an enclosed stairway down to the lower level of the house. I felt stupid, as well as fat, until I realized that the door to the guest powder room led off the main hallway in the approximate location where such an interior stair might be. I was right: inside the tiny powder room, which I'd seen but never actually entered before, there was another door in the wall opposite the sink. It was a skinny door like that of a closet, but when I opened it I saw a narrow, very steep flight of stairs going down.

I found a light switch just inside the doorjamb. Illuminated, the stairs looked less dangerous but still… I drew back and checked the door. Yes, there was a deadbolt lock, the kind with no latch to throw, requiring a key to lock or unlock it from either side.

I frowned as I carefully went down the steep stairs, not sure whether I was frowning at myself or at the situation. Was this stairway really a potential danger to our overmedicated residents? Should the door be kept locked? Or, since the door was in such a hard to find location anyway, was it really safer to leave the door unlocked at all times? At least that way, if residents did go down here, they couldn't lock themselves in by mistake.

When I reached the bottom of the stairs I felt oppressed by the atmosphere of this gloomy place. Practically speaking, I knew that I could turn on an overhead light, dispel the gloom, find the exercise equipment and get on with it, but I didn't. Nor could I say exactly why I didn't. I simply stood there at the bottom of those killer stairs and let my eyes adjust to the lack of light while I felt the weight of the great house over my head.

I was approximately in the center of a vast but not empty space. Huge square support pillars loomed in the semidarkness. Boxes, and shapes I couldn't identify, crowded among the pillars. The very air felt thick with dust and desertion. It was hard to breathe and hard to see—what faint light there was filtered murkily from too few windows at either end.

"Hell is murky," I muttered, and then tried to remember the source of the quote while I felt around on the wall for the light switch. Shakespeare, of course. Lady Macbeth, stumbling around in the gloom and doom, losing her mind. How appropriate!

"That's better!" I said aloud when a whole row of overhead lights flipped on, obedient to the touch of my fingers. A heck of a lot easier to dispel gloom now than it had been back in Shakespeare's day! Now the place just looked like a mess of boxes and old furniture and discarded household equipment—and off a short jog to my left was the exercise room. Its walls had been built of fiberboard and it looked jerry-built from the outside.

But not from the inside. Inside, the Masonite walls were sparkling white and looked spanking brand-new. All the equipment Sally had mentioned was there, and so were the mirrors, and everything gleamed. I walked around, touching shiny chrome surfaces and feeling slightly intimidated as I always did in such places. I peeked in the little glass window of the sauna, which looked much like a cedar closet to me. Sweating in a hot box was somehow not my idea of a good time, but to each his own. No lock on the sauna door, I registered—good.

For the remaining twenty minutes of my lunch hour I dutifully pedaled the exercise bike. It was top of the line, the kind that works arms as well as legs, and I felt as virtuous as I could have hoped for by the time I was through. Turning out lights as I headed back, I decided that my qualms about the residents having constant, unsupervised access to this room had probably been foolish. No doubt the room had been put in this out-of-the-way place on purpose. Anyone, resident or staff, would have to be highly motivated in order to run the gauntlet of creepiness involved in getting in and out of here....

At the top of the narrow stairway I grabbed the doorknob. It turned in my hand, but the door didn't open. I pulled; the door didn't budge. My heart seemed to skip a beat. I pushed on the door, thinking maybe I'd remembered wrong and it opened in the other direction, but it still didn't budge. My heart now raced, and rose up into my throat.

I don't have claustrophobia, not really—but I don't take kindly to being trapped in tight spaces, either. This stairway, enclosed between the very walls of the house, was a tight space indeed. I yanked and yanked on the door until my hands, now slick with cold sweat, slipped off the metal knob. Locked, no doubt about it. Somebody had locked me in!

"Okay, okay," I muttered, backing off. I turned and went back down the stairs. I had to hang on to my nerves to keep from running. If I went down those steep steps as fast as I wanted to, I'd break my neck— or at least an ankle. There had to be another way out. There was bound to be an outside door.

There was. In fact, there were doors big enough to drive a truck—or a carriage, as had once no doubt been the case—through, but both of these doors were also locked. I looked at my watch. I was now seven minutes late returning from my lunch break. Would anyone even notice? I doubted it.

I sat down on a dusty wooden packing case and rubbed at my temples. I didn't like to feel trapped and I did feel trapped, so it was hard to think clearly. The inevitable question—why would anybody lock me down here?—was irrelevant for the moment. How to get out was relevant.

I looked at the huge double door in front of me. I figured it would be directly beneath the Hall's front porch. In the walls on either side were windows whose dirty glass panes were the source of the murky light I'd noticed earlier. If this was my house, I thought, I'd hide a key to that big door somewhere down here. I got up to look for such a key, even though the thought of running my hands over dirty, cobwebby surfaces didn't appeal to me. I made a face. My white uniform wasn't likely to stay white much longer.

I didn't find a key anywhere near that big double door. So I worked my way through piles of boxes and assorted junk to the corresponding door at the back of the house and looked there, too, for a key. No luck. My fingernails had grit underneath them from the search, and my temper was worse than gritty. At least I wasn't panicky anymore, I was just plain angry at whoever had shut me in!

Once again I backed off and tried to think straight. Most likely Frances Stark—who else could it be?—had chosen this particular afternoon to decide that the access to the lower level of the house should be limited, and by accident locked me in. A fitting coincidence, since I was the person with all the objections about unsupervised access. Briefly I wondered if somebody could be trying to teach me a lesson; then I dismissed that line of thought as mild paranoia. Not only that, but a waste of time.

I made my way back to the stairs and sat at the bottom, thinking. I had two choices now: I could either go back up to the top of these stairs and pound on the door and yell for someone to let me out, which had the drawback of possibly frightening any residents who might hear me; or I could break one of the windows, which had the drawback of destroying property. Easy choice—I'd break the window.

I'd started off through the rows of boxes when I heard a thin, high voice calling "Hello-o-o! Hello down there!"

The voice was almost lost in all the vast space, and I didn't recognize it immediately.

"Hello-o-o?"

"Miss Lilibet!" I yelled. I turned and hurried as fast as I could back to the stairs. All I could think of was that tiny old woman losing her footing and tumbling, ending in a broken heap at the bottom of the killer stairs.

Make that tiny, sure-footed old woman. She looked completely out of place in one of her lace dresses, dripping with her habitual pearls, and I'd seldom been more glad to see anyone in my life.

"I thought you might be down here, Amanda," she said.

"You were right, as usual." I beamed at her, wanting to give her a bear hug like the ones I gave Sam, but I didn't dare. I settled for asking, "How did you know? And what's more important, how did you get the door unlocked?"

She was looking all around her with great interest. She ignored my questions, at least for the moment. I'd learned that Lilibet paid attention to precisely what she wanted, when she wanted, and I knew that if she wanted to answer me she'd get back to it. In her own time.

Now she wrinkled her dainty white nose and said, "I haven't been down here in a long time. Not since right after they put up that room with all the fancy machines. My goodness, somebody really needs to do some cleaning! I declare, I never did see a worse mess in my life!"

"Yes," I agreed. I started to take her arm but stopped myself—my hands were too dirty. Less direct methods were called for. "Uh, Lilibet, I really should get back to work. I didn't mean to be down here so long. So let's go back up together, shall we?"

"I suppose so. I don't much like it down here, anyway."

"I don't like the idea of you going up and down those steep stairs." I started in their direction, turned, waited for her to catch up.

Miss Lilibet slowly revolved, taking a parting look at the ground floor of Cottonwood Hall. She was frowning, shaking her head slightly. When she came abreast of me she stage-whispered, "*She* doesn't like it down here one bit, you know!"

"She?"

"The ghost."

"Oh, of course. You go on up the stairs first, Lilibet." If she stumbled, I could catch her.

"I know," she said pertly, chin in the air, "age before beauty!"

I rolled my eyes. "That's not what I meant, and you know it!"

She stepped onto the first step and then turned to me. Standing on the step made her eyes level with mine. "Why did you come down here today, Amanda?"

"I wanted to use the exercise bicycle on my lunch hour. Sally told me about the room and the equipment, and that anyone could use it. Somehow, I got locked in. Or at least I thought I was until you came, Miss Lilibet."

"Oh, the door was locked, all right. But I know where they keep the key." She reached under the ropes of pearls, into the bosom of her dress—hiding place of generations of women, present generation excepted—and pulled out a key. Her blue eyes glittered impishly. She stage-whispered again, "I snitched it. After I decided you must be down here, and I pulled on the door and it wouldn't open. I knew, you see, that it had to be locked if it wouldn't open."

"I will thank God for you every single day of my life, Miss Elizabeth Anne Bowe," I said solemnly.

"Oh, that's not really necessary, but I suppose it couldn't hurt!" With that she turned around and began a slow, careful ascent.

"Ahh," I said when we were almost to the top of the stairs, "you wouldn't happen to know who locked the door, or why, would you?"

"No, I surely don't." In the doorway she turned to me and said very sensibly, "But next time you go to ride the bicycle, if you feel you really must—I don't like to think of my favorite nurse going down in that awful place—next time you really should take the key with you, dear. Just in case.''

''I'm sure you're right. But you have an advantage over me, Lilibet. You know where it's kept, and I don't. I thought this door was never locked.''

''It's not supposed to be, not after what happened to poor Mr. Samuels last year.''

''What happened?''

''Oh, he had a little accident. He went in that hot-shower thing—''

''You mean the sauna?''

''If that's what you call it. Anyway, he went in that thing and he had a heart attack and couldn't get out, and nobody knew poor Mr. Samuels was down here, and somebody on the staff found the door unlocked and locked it back and so of course it was hours and hours before anybody found him.''

''That's terrible!'' And just precisely the kind of thing I'd been afraid might happen. Why, in God's name, didn't they just lock the place up for good instead of deciding the other way around, to leave it open all the time? All the time until today. It didn't make sense to me, but I didn't want to say so to Miss Lilibet.

She was whispering again. ''I'll tell you where they keep the key later on, Amanda. I have to be careful about putting it back, you know. Now you just get on about your business and we'll pretend none of this ever happened!''

My little old spy! I thought with a rush of affection as I watched her totter away, the picture of dotty innocence.

"YOU DIDN'T KEEP your office hours at the Hall last week, or this week," I said to Len. We sat on the side of the pool at his apartment complex, dangling our feet in the water and watching Samantha play in the shallow end. We had the whole pool to ourselves, probably because it was another gray day; but it was still hot, and Sam didn't object to the lack of sun—she would go in a swimming pool in pitch black dark if I'd let her.

"You noticed."

"Of course I noticed. We have patients, I mean residents, who need attention—"

"Did anybody ever tell you you can be a very exasperating woman at times, Amanda?" He said this affectionately, half-smiling, and his hair fell over one eye the way it often did. I knew, suddenly, who he reminded me of: Jeff Bridges, the actor. Len looked a lot like him, especially without a shirt. Or trousers. He was wearing a bathing suit, of course.

I nodded, fessing up. "Uh-huh. Doctors, mostly, when I went on about patients. And my husband, too...."

"Well, for your information, I did get over to the Hall to see the patients you're so concerned about, and all the rest of them. But I had to go at night, so you weren't there at the time. My life was sort of...messed up, I had things to take care of. In case you were hoping I lost my job at Cottonwood Hall, I didn't. I explained to the battle-ax, I mean Frances Stark, and she seemed to understand. I'll be there as scheduled from now on. I hope."

Now I remembered, Frances had said something about Len having problems. But I'd been too concerned about Tom Parker then to pay much attention. I glanced at Sam, saw that she was fine, and paid full if belated attention to Len.

"I'm sorry. You know I don't want you to lose your job at the Hall. Do you want to tell me what sort of problems?"

Len grinned. "Nope. I want to teach your daughter, the would-be fish, to swim. What do you think of that?"

"I think she'd love it!"

Sam did love it, she'd taken to Len right away. My daughter, usually so physically cautious, seemed to know that she could trust this big, gentle guy. I loved watching them together, splashing and kicking and shrieking with glee, both of them.

But I did wonder what Len's problems were, and if they were serious, and why he didn't want to tell me about them.

Chapter Eight

July dragged into August, which was the absolute worst month for weather as far as I was concerned. I thought half seriously about moving to Alaska. There was just one drawback to that, and it had nothing to do with ice and snow—Dr. Leonard Percy.

I was, as they say in the South, completely taken with him. I thought perhaps he felt the same about me. If our relationship didn't seem to be making much progress, that was as much my fault as his. He seemed to be too busy to spend the kind of time with me that had led to our one and only kiss, and I was content to go slowly. I seemed to have forgotten how to be close to anyone except my daughter. I had a score of acquaintances in Natchez, but no close friends. Nor, up until now, had I noticed the absence of friends in my life. Taking care of Samantha had been enough.

When I thought about it, I supposed I was just now coming out of a protracted period of grief. Taking the job at Cottonwood Hall had forced me to turn some sort of corner. Around that corner I'd found Len, and he was enough to keep me from moving to Alaska anytime soon.

So summer lumbered on, and if you didn't count my continuing concern about Magnus Everett and Tom Parker, things were quiet. The almost daily thunderstorms were less violent. I'd had no more phone calls from obscenely heavy breathers.

Then the new resident came to take Belinda's place. Her name was Anna Calvin White, and she was called Callie. She was forty-five, tall and thin with lank, longish blond hair fading to gray. Her eyes seemed faded, too, a watery pale blue. Because of her name, her unusually white skin and her thin, drooping posture, she reminded me of a calla lily. Her diagnosis was depression, and her medication was the highest dosage of the antidepressant Elavil that can be taken without serious side effects.

Callie attempted suicide on her second night at Cottonwood Hall. The night nurse didn't bother to tell me, I found out during my routine reading of the charts, which was always my first activity when I went on duty. The nurse's notes in Callie's chart said that she had broken the mirror in her room and attempted to slash her wrists with one of the pieces. The nursing assistant had heard the sound of the mirror breaking and had arrived in time to stop her. The nurse herself had not observed the "accident." She had not filed an Incident Report, as would have been required in other places I'd worked. I doubted that Cottonwood Hall had ever heard of Incident Reports.

I flipped to the back of the chart and checked Callie's medication record. In addition to the regular

Elavil, she'd been given what I considered a hefty dose of secobarbital, for sleep. There was no notation as to which doctor had ordered it, no indication that Dr. Leonard Percy had even been called. I put the chart back on the shelf and went to check on Callie—another person who in my opinion should be called a patient rather than a resident of Cottonwood Hall.

Callie White did not look as if she were sleeping, she looked as if she were dead. Her skin was whiter than the cream-colored background of her blue-flowered sheets. The shadows under her closed eyes were an even darker blue than the flowers. I took her thin wrist between my fingers and felt her pulse. It was thin, thready, slow. Her skin was not simply cool, it was cold. Her respirations were also slow, but not—thank God—abnormally so. Nevertheless I wanted complete vital signs.

I went back to the half bath that had been converted to a nurse's station and got my stethoscope and a blood pressure cuff. I was aware that I hadn't greeted any of the other residents in my usual morning fashion, and from the corner of my eye I saw a couple of them standing in their doorways watching me. I let the bustle of my movements speak for me—see, I'm busy now—and hurried back to the sleeping Callie.

The blank wooden backing of the broken mirror stared facelessly at me as I strained to hear the sounds of the woman's life-blood. *Dub, dub, dub.* I watched the pressure indicator rise, hesitate, then slowly, steadily fall. I wrote the numbers in ink on the palm of my hand, a habit picked up long ago in nursing school, so that I wouldn't forget them before I got back to her chart. Callie's blood pressure was on the low side of normal. She was simply in a deep, deep sleep and would probably awake twelve to fourteen hours after the time she'd been given the secobarbital. If I remembered correctly, that had been a little after 2:00 a.m. She was likely to sleep through my entire shift.

Suddenly I sensed I was no longer alone. I looked up, startled by a little *frisson* my rational mind told me there was no reason for. I said, "Hello, Peter."

"'Lo." Peter Stephenson stood in the doorway. He had the deceptively youthful appearance that people who are both mentally ill and slightly retarded can often present—as long as they are well cared for. He was actually middle-aged but his round face was as smooth and unlined as a child's. He was also round-shouldered and round-bellied and with all that roundness you expected him to bounce when he walked, but he didn't, he shuffled. He hadn't dressed yet, which surprised me. He was wearing a plaid cotton flannel robe over pajamas, and slippers on his feet.

"Did you want to talk to me, Peter?" I asked, coming toward the door.

"Guess so." He shrugged. When I reached him he moved back.

"Shall we talk in your room?"

"Guess so."

This was surprising. Peter's diagnosis was schizoid personality, meaning that he was withdrawn and antisocial. That, combined with his mild retardation, made him unable to function on his own in the real world. It also meant that here, where all his needs were met, he seldom spoke at all. Certainly he'd never voluntarily spoken to me before. He returned to his own room like a plump homing pigeon, only with a shuffle rather than a strut.

Peter shuffled to one of two chairs by his window, and I sat in the other. "Okay..." I ventured.

He frowned, puckering his smooth skin. His plump fingers picked at the cloth of the robe upon his thighs. When at last he raised his eyes to me, I was shocked by their expression. It was fear. He said, "She scream. New lady scream, try to hurt herself."

"Last night," I agreed, nodding. "But this is today, and she's all right. She didn't hurt herself. She's sleeping, and when she wakes up she'll be fine." I'd had no previous experience with patients like Peter, and I wasn't sure how much he was capable of understanding.

The pucker on his face smoothed out, but there was still fear in his eyes. And his fingers still plucked, plucked at the robe. "Just like the other time. The other time. That lady's gone. She's dead. We saw her in the cof-cof-coffin."

"This is different, Peter—" I began to reassure him, but stopped myself. I'd always believed in telling the truth to patients; or if the truth was beyond their comprehension, at the very least not lying to them. So I changed my tack. "Did the noise wake you up last night, is that what happened? She screamed, and it scared you?"

"Guess so."

"Tell me what you remember, please. Try to tell me."

"Dark. Noise. Screaming. Broke-broke-broken g-glass."

"You heard the glass break?" Somehow I'd assumed that was what had awakened him. "You mean first you heard screams and then after that you heard the glass break?"

"Guess so. Sh-shad-shad-shadows. Shadows, too." There was so much fear in Peter's round eyes now that he looked wild. Desperate. And I felt desperately sorry for him.

"Shadows can be frightening, but it's all over now. There's nothing more to worry about, Peter. No shadows on a day like today, see?" I leaned and stretched my arm toward the window, pulling the sheer curtain aside so that sunlight flooded the room.

Peter looked out at the sunlight, then back toward the hall. "Guess not," he said. I knew this was his way of refusing, because it was what he said when he didn't want to take his medication.

That reminded me—I hadn't given any of the residents their morning meds yet. Today Peter certainly needed the tranquilizer prescribed for him, whereas on other days I had often wondered and just as often allowed him to refuse it. I should get back to my routine, but before I did I wanted to ask one more question.

"What do you mean, Peter, you guess not?"

He turned his head, his eyes so full of fear staring into mine. "Some-some-something bad come. In dark. Bad. Ladies scream. Die. Dead in cof-cof-coffin. Peter a-a-afraid."

I took both his hands in mine and felt how they trembled when I stopped their plucking motion. "You haven't had your medication yet this morning, and that's my fault," I said. "I'm going to get it now, and after you take it you'll feel much better."

I hated the sound of my own voice, inadequate, placating. But I left Peter and then one by one I gave all the residents their medication. I didn't know what else to do.

Sometime between one and three that afternoon, Magnus Everett died. Quietly. In his sleep.

TWO DAYS LATER I sat, by my own request, in Frances Stark's office. Len Percy was also present. I hadn't told him ahead of time what I intended to do, but I'd left a message with his answering service that this meeting was to occur, so perhaps he'd invited himself. Sally was probably all ears on the other side of the flimsy divider wall. That was fine with me. Except that it would have upset them, I wouldn't have cared if every patient—yes, *patient!*!—in Cottonwood Hall was right there in the room with us.

"It is not unexpected for a new patient to go down at first," said Frances from behind her gleaming mahogany desk.

"You mean decompensate?" asked Len, leaning forward.

She nodded. "Yes."

I regarded the slightly scuffed toes of my white shoes with deep concentration. I noticed that my sheer white stockings had a pulled place on the right ankle, which would doubtless soon become a run. An uncomfortable silence fell. I let it, studying my shoes even harder. I'd said everything I had to say at this point about Callie White. This was only the beginning. I had other, uglier stuff to bring up and I was already wanting to run screaming out among the cottonwoods. I didn't want either of them to know that.

Len picked up the ball, either out of consideration for me or because he had stuff of his own to deal with and my suddenly requested conference had given him his opportunity.

"I presume," he said to Frances, "that Miss White came with more previous records than what you have placed in her chart."

"I don't believe so. No. She was not in an institution prior to coming here. She was at home, she lived with her mother."

I looked up. This was news to me. This, certainly, was not in the chart. "What happened? Why did her mother decide she could no longer take care of Callie?"

Frances's face was as devoid of expression as a mask. "Her mother died. I do not know the details, I know only that we had an opening, I was contacted on Miss White's behalf, and she fit our guidelines for admission."

"I was not consulted," said Len, with an authority in his voice I admired.

Frances turned her face to him, showing her hatchetlike profile to me. It had been perfectly obvious ever since my first day at the Hall that she did not like Len. I'd never yet been able to figure out why.

"It has never been our policy to contact the staff psychiatrist about admissions. Your predecessor would not have been contacted. The administrator is the admissions officer, Dr. Percy. I did not ignore you or neglect you out of some whim or concern for your relative youth and inexperience."

"I did not mean to suggest that you did, Mrs. Stark." Len colored slightly and leaned back in his chair.

Probably forcing himself to relax, I thought. But my instincts had grabbed hold of me and I pounced. "Is that your policy for Cottonwood Hall, Frances?" I deliberately used her first name, to remind her that she'd once thought enough of me to invite me to do so. Then I pushed on, "Or is it the policy of the Cypress Group for all their rest homes?"

I felt sudden, intense attention from Len, but I didn't glance his way. I kept my eyes on Frances, fascinated by the process going on within her. She didn't move a muscle on the surface, yet she was turning to stone from the inside out. She radiated coldness, hardness.

Finally her voice cut through the air. "How do you know of our affiliation with the Cypress Group?"

I lied, because I could see this was serious and I didn't want to get Sally into trouble. "I don't recall, I've just always known, that's all."

"It is not common knowledge."

"I've never heard of the Cypress Group," said Len.

"The Cypress Group is exceedingly discreet," said Frances to both of us, measuring every word, "due to the nature of their clientele. You must not speak of this again outside this room. Do you understand? You have somehow, Amanda, gained access to privileged information and I suggest that you forget it.''

"Maybe I will, once you've answered my question,'' I said boldly. Perhaps foolishly.

"The administrator, that is myself, makes all decisions except in a potentially life-threatening situation. In which case the medical doctor, the psychiatrist, is called. This is not an unusual policy, I believe the same is true in virtually any nursing home or rest home.''

I persisted, "Callie White tried to commit suicide her second night here, and nobody called Dr. Percy. You don't consider that life-threatening?''

"I must presume you have a good reason for being so challenging, Amanda.'' I could see that Frances was struggling to keep her good opinion of me. There were cracks in her stone facade. "So I will reiterate, Miss White decompensated slightly, *after* her admission. She did not succeed in her suicide attempt—if indeed that is what it was. She does not even remember it now. Her life is in no danger.''

No, I thought, she just hallucinates and babbles and most of the time doesn't know where she is. But I knew I'd pushed Frances hard enough on that point.

Len shifted in his chair and said, "Ah—''

"All right, I'll concede that,'' I said swiftly, not giving Len a chance. "My next concern—you recall, Frances, when I asked for this meeting I said I had several concerns—''

She nodded.

"—and the next one is Magnus Everett, who died two days ago. His body was gone yesterday morning when I came to work. What happened to him? Will there be an autopsy, a funeral, a cremation, what?"

"I don't understand why this is of concern to you," said Frances.

"No autopsy. I didn't ask for one," Len explained. "Didn't see any need. The man was ancient, his physical health hadn't been good since that episode a few weeks ago—"

"He slept too much," I put in.

Len glanced at me in consternation, "We were keeping him comfortable. Anyway, with his mental health long gone and recently his physical health, too, I considered his death a blessing. I would have thought you'd feel the same, Amanda. And in case you're still wondering, he's already been cremated."

"Okay." I didn't bother to say that Magnus Everett hadn't had the kind of illness that requires total zonking out in order to be kept comfortable; nor did I say that I personally thought the amount of tranquilizer Len had prescribed for Magnus could not possibly have caused the man to sleep all day, every day for over three weeks. I went on to my next concern, instead. "Then what about Tom Parker?"

"The autistic young man?" Frances had thawed somewhat, she had an interested spark in her eyes.

"What about him?" asked Len.

"Why is he having hallucinations?"

There was a dead silence in the office. My heart thudded so hard I was surprised they couldn't hear it. I felt, not victory exactly, but deep satisfaction. Here was a fact I knew they did not know, and I felt they could not ignore. The kind of fact that must lead to some positive action.

But I was wrong.

Len said, "Autistics don't have hallucinations."

Frances said, "I concur."

I said, "I know he's having them. I was with him yesterday when one occurred. He doesn't act like a typical autistic anymore. The trouble is, nobody seems to have noticed it except me."

"I have to question your powers of observation, Amanda," Frances said.

Len shifted in his chair so that he faced me. "I, uh, I hate to say this, Amanda, but so do I."

I WOULD NOT SEE Len when I got off work that day, even though he more than asked, he practically begged me to. I said I couldn't, that I had to pick up Sam— which was true, but I also was taking her to a friend's house to play for the rest of the afternoon and then have supper. I was free, and under other circumstances I would have had a lot to discuss with Len. But not now, not anymore. After the way he'd practically turned against me right in front of Frances, I didn't think I'd ever want to talk to him again!

I dropped Sam off at her friend's house and drove aimlessly for a while. I went out into the country, on blacktop roads from whose hot surface waves of heat rose like shimmering transparent wraiths. Little dips in the road that would have been invisible in cooler weather turned to silver mirages only to disappear as soon as I approached.

The inside of my car was cool from the blessed air-conditioning. The insides of me were boiling. I wasn't sure how many miles I'd driven before I was calm enough to think more or less straight.

Maybe I was wrong about Tom Parker. He'd had to be kept on heavy tranquilizers since his head-banging episode. I'd seen for myself that when we reduced the dose, he went back into the violent rocking that presaged more head banging. I admitted, grudgingly, that the only things I knew about autistics were what I had learned in books. I'd never in all my years as a military nurse had a real live patient like Tom.

I topped another gentle rise, descended into another silver puddle of mirage that disappeared without a splash. What if the autistic person's inner world was not as silent as it appeared to us on the outside? What if such a person always had a kind of hallucination going on, but day to day simply lacked whatever mental connection was necessary to react to it? What if the heavy tranquilizer—in Tom's case Thorazine—somehow broke through the autistic's silent facade and allowed an observable reaction to occur?

I had observed something. I'd been with Tom, seen him start to roll back and forth on his bed and vocalize. I'd watched his eyes. He was seeing something, I'd been sure of it, something that wasn't really there. I had called that a hallucination. I still had trouble calling it anything else.

The problem was, I didn't know what this meant. My own head ached with trying to sort out what was real from what was not real. Tom Parker might have been seeing something he saw all the time, something that was real and usual to him. Was that a hallucination, or wasn't it?

What about Callie? She most definitely was hallucinating, every day. Decompensation? Yes, severely depressed patients can hallucinate. I knew that.

Okay, what about poor dead Belinda? She had hallucinated, too, and hadn't been conscious afterward to tell anyone about it. Magnus Everett? The day he'd gone naked into the hall in a thunderstorm he had been hallucinating. He identified something, some part of the content of his hallucination as "bad." Not just bad, but "bad-bad-bad-bad-bad."

And finally Peter. Totally unimaginative, slow-witted Peter, said that bad things come in the night. In the dark, he'd said.

Was I going crazy myself, or was there really and truly something strange—strange, hallucination provoking, and life threatening—going on at Cottonwood Hall?

I knew what my faithful spy, Lilibet, would say— it's the ghost. I could believe in ghosts. I did believe, strongly, that hallucinations *are* reality for those having them. Suffering from them. Yes, our patients at the Hall were most definitely suffering, and some had died. And in my heart, in my gut, I knew that more would die.

There has to be a pattern, I thought, there must be a reason. This is not, cannot be, just a consequence of their mental illnesses. Something else is going on here!

It was time to turn the car around and head back. I glanced at my watch. Past time. I would have to look for a gas station where I could call my daughter and tell her that I might be late.

THERE WAS TIME, since I'd reached Samantha and found her in no hurry to be picked up, for me to stop at my favorite place overlooking the river. I'd driven the last few miles into an increasingly beautiful sunset, row on row of long, low-lying horizontal clouds that had changed from gold to orange to pink, and now were shading into deepest rose tinged with purple. I drove as close to the edge of the bluff as I dared, then stopped the car and got out.

The heat hit me like a moist blast furnace, but for once I didn't care. I couldn't see the river if I stayed in the car, and the sight was worth almost any discomfort. That broad, majestically pulsing band of water reflected the sky's splendor. I gasped as suddenly the sinking sun burst through the long lines of clouds, blazing scarlet. Huge and blindingly beautiful. The red sun lit the water like a running line of fire. Dying in glory.

"So you come here, too. Somehow that doesn't surprise me."

The voice was Len's, and startled me because I hadn't heard anyone approach. I stiffened, I clenched my hands into fists. I didn't turn around.

"I'm glad you're here," he said.

And then something happened—something odd, and totally unexpected.

Chapter Nine

Len touched my arm, just the merest, lightest touch, and that touch ran like a line of fire along my skin, just as the setting sun had sent its fire running along the river. I had not expected to feel this way—I thought it was odd when only minutes before I'd been angry with him.

I said his name—"Len." No more than that because my eyes pricked with tears. I dared not turn to him because I didn't want him to see.

"Amanda." His voice was husky, deep with emotion. He was standing close behind me and I felt him step closer; I knew we were only inches apart. He spoke again. "I went to your house, sat in my car and waited for you to come. Waited and waited. I couldn't stand what I knew you must be thinking of me. I wanted to explain, but you weren't there so I couldn't, and the longer I waited the more I simply couldn't stand even the thought of being without you. Your house looked so empty. The whole town felt empty, *I* felt empty, and still you didn't come. Finally I left. Finding you here is like a miracle."

I let myself lean back against him, wordlessly. I closed my eyes, knowing that they brimmed with tears—tears of relief: He felt so strong, so solid as his arms closed around me. He bent his head and placed his cheek next to mine, pulling me more firmly into his embrace. The fire ignited by that first touch now burned with a steady, pure flame that was not desire but something different. Deeper than desire.

"I'm glad you're here," I said.

He turned me slowly, gently around, keeping me in the circle of his arms. I looked up at his face and saw there serious lines of wanting, underscored by longing in his eyes. With one hand he cradled my head. My lips parted, I yearned for his kiss. And Len kissed me.

It was a kiss of such transforming power that it took our breaths away and left us standing astonished in the deepening twilight. It was a kiss that taught a lesson: See, you are each fine and strong when you are alone, but together you have strength to move the world!

Other kisses followed—exploring, reassuring. With each meeting of lips, each touch of tongues we learned that the power, the new power of *us,* was real.

When at last I stood back and so did Len, our hands linked, the words that came out of my mouth sounded ridiculous.

I said, "I was so angry with you."

He cocked his head, that endearing grin on his face, and said, "I guess you're not mad anymore."

I laughed, and swung our hands for joy. "No, I'm not!" My heart was singing. "But I do have to go and pick up my daughter."

"Mind if I follow you?"

"I'd be disappointed if you didn't." Hands still joined, we turned our backs to the river, which rolled on like an eternal promise.

WHILE I PUT Samantha to bed, Len went out for Chinese food since neither of us had eaten.

"I like Len a lot," said my daughter. "Is he going to be my daddy now?"

For a minute I felt as if she'd hit me between the eyes. I said cautiously, "You already have a daddy, sweetheart, even if he died and can't be with us. You know that, you've seen his picture and you know that you look just exactly like him."

She snuggled her head into the pillow, getting comfortable, then blinked her wide, innocent eyes. "I know, but he's gone to another world and we're here, and Len's here and I like him, and so do you. I can tell."

I smoothed her springy auburn curls, smiling at the unshakableness of her child's logic. "Yes, I do like him, and I'm glad you do, too. Len is a friend, Samantha."

"He's my friend, too, he said so," she told me drowsily. She'd had a long day, played hard, and her eyes were already at half-mast.

I kissed her velvety cheek. "Yes, he's a good friend to both of us. You go on to sleep now, honey. We'll talk more tomorrow. Good night."

"Good night, Mommy." Her brown lashes, so thick they were like fur, fluttered down upon her cheeks and I tiptoed away. But when I was at her door I heard her say dreamily, "Friends make the very best daddies."

"YOU'VE WON my daughter's heart."

"Well, the feeling is mutual. She's a great kid, Amanda. Not to mention smart!"

"I know," I said, polishing off the last of the fried rice on my plate. "Sometimes she's so smart for her age it almost scares me."

"You've done a great job and I know it can't have been easy for you, taking care of her alone." Len said this carefully, not looking at me, concentrating instead on the process of spooning what remained of the sweet-and-sour pork from the carton onto his plate.

We hadn't talked much while we ate. We'd moved into new territory and we both knew it. Little glances, brief touches, small smiles all acknowledged the tender newness in our relationship. And I still carried inside myself a completely new thought implanted there by my daughter less than an hour before: Samantha wanted a father—that was one thing that had never, ever occurred to me.

I picked up a fortune cookie but didn't break it open; I turned it around and around, as if the answers to everything were wrapped up inside but I wasn't ready for them yet. Looking at the cookie I said, "Thank you. The truth is, it wasn't really hard."

"No?"

"I, ah, I don't know how to explain this to someone who doesn't have any children—"

"I have brothers and sisters, and a whole army of cousins. Try me."

So, that was how he came to be so good with children! I smiled. "Okay. It's like Sam was born already being this fascinating little person. I was completely wrapped up in her from the very first. Everything she did was so interesting...." I let my voice trail off, lost in memories.

Len allowed the silence.

Finally, a little dazed and embarrassed, I snapped back to the present and looked at him. "I don't mean that physically it wasn't difficult at times. The getting up in the night and all that—there was a time when I felt like I'd been tired for years. But the physical part didn't seem so important, not compared to, to—" I lost my words.

"To the loneliness you would have felt without her," said Len softly, leaning toward me across the table.

"I wasn't lonely!" I snapped.

"Yes, you were. You must have been."

"How would you know?" I glared at him. "And why would you have to say something like that, anyway?"

"I'm a psychiatrist, Amanda." Len shrugged, and leaned back. "I can't help it. I see how brave you are, what a determined fighter you are, and I have a hunch how you got to be that way. Don't get me wrong, I admire you for it."

I felt the tension drain out of me. "I've always been more or less a fighter, it didn't come with single motherhood." I put the fortune cookie down, surprised I hadn't broken it to bits.

"Um-hmm."

"Anyway, I've never thought it was hard taking care of Samantha by myself. What has been hard is going back to work, having Sam in daycare. I know it's the right thing, really, even if I didn't need the money.'' For some reason, I couldn't look at Len while I was talking about this. I stood up and stacked dishes and empty cartons while I continued. ''She needs more time with children her own age. One reason she seems so smart is that she's spent so much time exclusively with me.''

''Um-hmm.''

''I wish you'd stop that!'' I marched from the kitchen table to the counter with my load of dishes.

''Stop what?''

''That um-hmming. It makes you sound like a psychiatrist, and makes me feel like you're trying to analyze me or something.''

''I'm sorry. I just have this uncontrollable desire to understand what makes people tick. Especially you.''

Um-hmm, I thought, but at least I didn't say it. I turned the water on to rinse the dishes before putting them in the dishwasher—I know you're not supposed to have to, but somehow I can never make myself believe it. Len, quietly helpful, brought the glasses and gathered up the cartons off the counter and found the trash basket all by himself. I thought, *This is necessary, this kind of talk. So why do I feel so defensive?*

Then, slightly stunned, I stood at the sink with my hands under the running water and realized that Len was right. I had been lonely. For five years I'd lived in perfect denial of my own loneliness.

As he passed by on his way back to the table, I snagged his sleeve. Looking up at him I said very quietly, ''If I ever criticize you again for sounding like a psychiatrist, I hope you'll give me a good swift kick.''

He quirked one eyebrow, and his mouth on that same side, a characteristic look. "What brought that on?"

"You're good, Doctor. You were right. Emotionally it was hard taking care of Samantha alone."

"I'm sure it was." Len backed me against the counter, reached his long arm around me and turned off the water. "You're a strong woman, Amanda."

"No, I'm not." I shook water from my fingertips, and also shook my head.

"Yes, you are." Len leaned with his hands on the counter on either side of me, trapping me within his arms. "Sometimes you're so strong it scares me."

"Why?" My voice was just above a whisper as I searched deep within his eyes, a little frightened by the depth of feeling I saw there.

"Because I know you can survive very well without me, and I'm not so sure anymore that I would want to survive without you." His lips closed over mine. His body pressed against me and I felt the urgency with which he wanted me.

I melted against him, felt my body become all softness, molding to his hardness. I was the lock, he was the key. My arms circled his broad shoulders and when his lips left mine I buried my hand in his hair to keep his head next to mine. I whispered, my lips at his ear, "I don't want to be alone anymore."

WE DID NOT make love. Perhaps we would have if there hadn't been a sleeping four-year-old in the house. Or perhaps not. At midnight after Len had left, I sat on the side of the bed brushing my hair, which he'd taken down earlier, and thinking about our not making love. What we had done instead had been nice— very, very nice.

I brushed long, languorous strokes. I was glad to be a human being, glad to have a body with hair and skin and eyes and lips and tongue and exquisite nerve endings virtually everywhere. Glad to have a mind, so that I could value and remember every part of what had happened since I'd stopped on the bluff to watch that most beautiful of sunsets.

I compared Len to Sam, and that didn't seem a bad thing to do. It seemed natural, not demeaning to either of them. Len was different from my husband, a very different kind of man. Len made me think about a song from years ago, about a man with slow hands, a lover with an easy touch. I had a glimmer of understanding about myself with Len: I'd been taught to love by my husband, who had been swift, passionate and powerful, and I'd learned to catch fire quickly in response. Thus, the sudden flaring of desire I'd felt for Len.

But his style was different, and in his hands my flaring spark became a spreading glow, a steadily growing flame. Len gentled me with his own gentleness, tempered me with his tenderness. He had such depth, and I was sure that when the time came for us to join our bodies, I would find Len no less powerful than Sam had been.

I put my brush back on the dresser, shrugged out of my robe, got into bed and turned off the bedside lamp. Then, finally, I thought about the talking Len and I had done. Later, when touching and kissing had become almost more torment than pleasure.

Len had turned suddenly grave, and said it was time he gave me the explanation I deserved for his seeming to side with Frances Stark against me. He said he'd only done that so that I wouldn't say any more in front of her, because he had a strong hunch that if there was something going on, as he put it "detrimental to the welfare of the patients," Frances was likely to be in on it. He hadn't liked that business about the Cypress Group and keeping it all hush-hush, and he said he intended to find out more about them. I'd admitted that it was Sally who told me but I hadn't wanted to get her in trouble, and I told him everything else I could remember of what she'd said.

Len asked me if I had any ideas about what could be causing these patient problems, and I'd admitted that I didn't have a clue, only a lot of concerns. Then we'd both tossed around ideas without getting anywhere, and agreed that the essential first step would be to get access to their complete records. That would be difficult to do without Frances knowing, but Len said he'd try to think of a legitimate way to get them without arousing suspicion.

I'd challenged him, my old fighting spirit returning, with *Why can't you just assert yourself and say that you want the records, you're the doctor for heaven's sake!* And with a rueful grin, running his hand through his hair and mussing it up, he'd said that considering all the patients he'd lost out of his new private practice, if he did anything that cost him the staff position at the Hall he wouldn't have any choice but to leave Natchez.

Then, at last, Len had told me about those problems of his own that he wouldn't talk about before. I had to admit it was serious. Somebody had been spreading rumors, telling tales about him. Particularly nasty, vicious tales that he didn't want to tell me the content of until I insisted. Someone had started the rumor that Len Percy had engaged in intercourse and other sex acts with his patients when he was a resident psychiatrist in Jackson.

I lay in bed and thought how horrible that was, how impossible to defend himself against such a vicious charge, particularly when it wasn't even out in the open but just whispered about. He'd gone to Dr. Stewart as soon as one of his patients was loyal enough to disbelieve and to tell Len. Then he'd also gone to Jackson and talked to the man who'd been his attending psychiatrist when he was a resident. Both had advised him to say nothing, ride it out if he could and if he couldn't, to leave and start over again somewhere else.

I turned over, feeling suddenly lonely in my double bed, wishing that Len was with me and that I knew how to comfort him. Of course he'd never done such a thing. He was a kind, gentle man, sensitive, caring....

Close to sleep now, I thought how selfish I'd been to keep insisting that Len pay attention to my relatively petty concerns about the people at Cottonwood Hall. Only to me they didn't seem petty....

With visions moving behind my closed eyes, of Callie and Tom and poor dead Magnus, poor dead Belinda, of Miss Lilibet walking and stalking a ghost, I fell asleep.

I DREAMED. I had one of those awful nights where you wake yourself up out of a bad dream, only to fall asleep right back into it again. I dreamed of Belinda in her open coffin with the candles burning at her head and feet. I dreamed that I was locked into Cottonwood Hall and couldn't get out. Like Miss Lilibet but without her patient acceptance, I walked and walked halls that had become as tall as the inside of a cathedral, with doors that were yawning black spaces until I approached them, and then one of the residents would pop up in the blackness, face distorted by madness and spouting gibberish as Magnus had done.

I dreamed of black riders—whatever they had been to Magnus, in my dream they were black-cloaked and hooded, with silver glowing eyes, mounted on horses from hell. I dreamed of Callie, rising from her bed like a vampire from a coffin, tall and wraithlike, holding a calla lily to her breast. Her eyes burned like coals.

I dreamed of Sally Creech and Frances Stark, looking like themselves but both stalking me, intent on doing me harm. Finally I dreamed that Miss Lilibet was lost somewhere in the Hall, and I was looking for her. Calling and calling and calling. It was night and I couldn't find her; the whole house was dark. Outside I could hear the cottonwood trees talking to each other in their restless murmurs, and I opened the French doors and went out onto the porch. Outside it was pitch black dark, and in that dark there suddenly loomed a stark white face, no longer human, its mouth a soundlessly screaming *O*. And it had burning eyes. . . .

I woke up snatching at the air for breath, my heart pounding, my fingers knotted in the sheet so tightly there was pain. Gradually I realized that I was safe in my own bed and the night was over, the pearl gray of predawn light was spreading across the ceiling. I felt as if I hadn't slept at all but I got up anyway. The afterimage of that white, inhuman face was burned into my mind; I couldn't shake it. When I went into the bathroom I didn't dare to look into the mirror for fear I would see that *thing* instead of myself.

Of course I knew where I'd seen it before, and not since—on the porch my first day at Cottonwood Hall. Was that the ghost Miss Lilibet was always talking about?

I mulled this over while I made coffee and from my kitchen window watched the sun come up. Perhaps I was too much influenced by a night full of bad dreams, but I decided that it was time I learned more about the history of this house called Cottonwood Hall. In particular, if there were any ghost stories about the place. Len could handle the more scientific stuff, like getting access to charts and interpreting them. I was going to find out if any of our hallucinating residents really could be seeing a ghost!

ON SATURDAY MORNING Samantha and I went to the public library. I left her in the children's room, happily ensconced among a pile of books for beginning readers, and I went upstairs to the history section—local history in particular. I expected to have to dig—Natchez history had fascinated me ever since I'd moved here, and I couldn't remember ever having seen anything about a house called Cottonwood Hall.

Computerization hadn't yet reached the Natchez Public Library, so I did my research the old-fashioned way, with the subject index of the card catalog. I tried every cross-reference I could think of and got nowhere. I went to the shelves and pulled out books of Natchez town houses and plantation houses and checked their indexes. Ditto. I was beginning to feel as if my dreams were the reality, that I'd been living in them, that Cottonwood Hall didn't really exist. It was frustrating, and decidedly weird.

After checking on Sam, and finding that she had joined a group of children being entertained by a storyteller, I went to the reference librarian and explained my problem.

"Cottonwood Hall?" She shook her head, and my stomach went all hollow at the look of disbelief on her face. She said, "I don't know of any of our old homes by that name. Are you sure?"

"I'm not only sure, I work there every day. It's been turned into a kind of rest home."

She still looked doubtful. "Where, exactly, is it?"

I told her, and was vastly relieved to see a light of recognition in her eyes. "I remember now, some people bought the old Everhard plantation, not too far back. Less than ten years ago, it was, and I heard they intended to do something commercial with it." Her nose wrinkled in distaste, but she went on. "The

Everhards were always a reclusive bunch, stayed out of the mainstream of Natchez society or else they'd never have done such a thing. I doubt we'll have much but there is this one book..."

I sat down at a table with the one book. It was a thin book of unmanageably large dimensions, a folio-size volume full of black-and-white photographs that had been taken just after the Second World War. The text read as if it had been written by someone educated in Victorian times, or at least to Victorian standards. Its subject was not Natchez, but great plantations of south Mississippi. And there was Everhard Plantation, aka Cottonwood Hall.

The "extensive grove of cottonwood trees surrounding the manor house" was mentioned, so I guessed the new owners—presumably the Cypress Group—had renamed the house for the trees. When this book was written the house had still been in the hands of the Everhard family. The old photographs were fascinating, and I had to admit that if you were willing to forgive the addition of the wing at the back, the Cypress Group had done a wonderful job of restoration. Cottonwood Hall was now obviously in better repair than it had been when the Everhards were in residence and these pictures had been taken. I read avidly, and learned that I'd been on target with my guesses about the stages in which the house had been built. Miss Lilibet—bless her!—had also been on target. There was a ghost.

And this was her story: Amelia Mason had married Lionel Everhard in 1851, and as the young couple had their children, they also built the magnificent Greek

Revival facade around the old Georgian-style manor house. A decade later Lionel became an officer in the Army of the Confederacy, and Amelia capably took over management of the plantation in his absence. When it became clear that the Union forces would either penetrate Natchez from the north or move upward from already occupied New Orleans, Amelia sent her children into the interior of the state, away from the river. Alone except for a few faithful servants, Amelia Everhard stayed to watch over the house.

A Confederate messenger arrived one day with fateful news: Lionel Everhard was dead, and Union soldiers were on the march toward Natchez. Amelia was advised to flee, but she stayed put. She would not leave the house she and her husband had so lovingly transformed. The servants ran away, but still she stayed on. Alone.

The reason so many of the great antebellum homes survived the Civil War relatively intact was that the Union used Natchez as a regional headquarters, and their officers commandeered the elegant houses for living space. When the blue-uniformed officers and men rode and marched up to Everhard, they found a defiant Amelia standing between the pillars at the top of the steps. She refused to leave.

They stabled their horses under the house, they moved in, and still she would not go. So the Captain confined Amelia to a room "on the second floor at the back of the house," and allowed her out only to cook and clean for them. *Belinda's room, now Callie's room,* I thought, and I felt shivery.

CASINO JUBILEE
"Scratch'n Match" Game

Here's how to play:

1. Peel off label from front cover. Place it in space provided at right. With a coin, carefully scratch off the silver box. This makes you eligible to receive two or more free books, and possibly another gift, depending upon what is revealed beneath the scratch-off area.

2. You'll receive brand-new Harlequin Intrigue® novels. When you return this card, we'll rush you the books and gift you qualify for, ABSOLUTELY FREE!

3. Then, if we don't hear from you, every month we'll send you 4 additional novels to read and enjoy. You can return them and owe nothing, but if you decide to keep them, you'll pay only $2.24* each plus 25¢ delivery and applicable sales tax, if any*. That's the complete price, and—compared to cover prices of $2.89 each in stores—quite a bargain!

4. When you join the Harlequin Reader Service®, you'll get our subscribers-only newsletter, as well as additional free gifts from time to time, just for being a subscriber!

5. You must be completely satisfied. You may cancel at any time simply by sending us a note or a shipping statement marked "cancel" or by returning any shipment to us at our cost.

YOURS FREE!

This lovely heart-shaped box is richly detailed with cut-glass decorations, perfect for holding a precious memento or keepsake—and it's yours absolutely free when you accept our no-risk offer.

CASINO JUBILEE
"Scratch'n Match" Game

SCRATCH HERE

PLACE LABEL HERE

?

CHECK CLAIM CHART BELOW FOR YOUR FREE GIFTS!

YES! I have placed my label from the front cover in the space provided above and scratched off the silver box. Please send me all the gifts for which I qualify. I understand I am under no obligation to purchase any books, as explained on the opposite page.

181 CIH AH2Y (U-H-I-03/93)

Name _____

Address _____ Apt. _____

City _____ State _____ Zip _____

 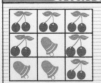
▼ DETACH AND MAIL CARD TODAY! ▼

HARLEQUIN ''NO RISK'' GUARANTEE

- You're not required to buy a single book—ever!
- You must be completely satisfied or you may cancel at any time simply by sending us a note or a shipping statement marked ''cancel'' or by returning any shipment to us at our cost. Either way, you will receive no more books; you'll have no obligation to buy.
- The free books and gift you claimed on the ''Casino Jubilee'' offer remain yours to keep no matter what you decide.

If offer card is missing, please write to: Harlequin Reader Service® P.O. Box 1867, Buffalo, N.Y. 14269-1867

▲ DETACH AND MAIL CARD TODAY! ▲

BUSINESS REPLY MAIL
FIRST CLASS MAIL   PERMIT NO. 717   BUFFALO, NY

POSTAGE WILL BE PAID BY ADDRESSEE

HARLEQUIN READER SERVICE
3010 WALDEN AVE
PO BOX 1867
BUFFALO NY 14240-9952

NO POSTAGE
NECESSARY
IF MAILED
IN THE
UNITED STATES

There were stories about how fiercely Amelia guarded her lovely home, how she threatened with a kitchen knife the officer who dropped cigar ash on her China carpet, how she fussed at the men who scuffed her hardwood floors with their boot heels. And at night, when they slept, she roamed the halls like a sentry for the house's sake. She never seemed to sleep.

Amelia lasted out the War and so did Everhard Plantation, though in greatly reduced circumstances. But when her children returned home they found that their mama had become a little strange. She paid very little attention to them, and seemed to care only about the house. She continued to dress in mourning, continued on living in that one room and walking the halls at night for all the rest of her life—and she lived to an old, old age. After her death many of her descendants and visitors to the house swore that she continued to walk the halls, vigilantly guarding her precious Everhard.

Whew! I thought, closing the book. I could almost see her, in her black dress with its great bell-shaped skirt, standing defiantly at the top of that long flight of steps. I could easily imagine her black-garbed figure swaying silently down the darkened halls at night. I wondered if she knew that the house no longer bore the much more distinguished name of Everhard, but was now called Cottonwood Hall. If she did, she wouldn't like it, that was for certain. Nor, I expected, would she approve of its housing such an odd assortment of people. On the other hand, she'd be able to see that the house itself was well cared for, and she might have sympathy for our residents, seeing as how she must have been more than a little out of her own mind....

"I'm ready to go now, Mommy." I had a fearless little female of my own here—four years old and she'd made her way through the big library and found me.

"Hi, sweetie. I guess you got tired of waiting for me. I'm sorry. I'm finished too, so we can go."

I returned the book, with thanks, to the librarian. Then I took Sam to her very favorite restaurant in the whole world, A Burger King restaurant, for lunch. While she ate and I drank my very favorite forbidden thing in the whole world, a chocolate milk shake, I wondered what I'd really accomplished. Okay, there was a solid basis for believing there might be a ghost at Cottonwood Hall. Lilibet would be glad to hear it, and the ghost's story if she didn't already know it. But as for me, I didn't feel any better for knowing. I could and did admire a woman like Amelia Everhard. But still, whenever I thought of a real ghost walking the halls where I walked, I felt my flesh creep along my bones.

GHOSTS MIGHT or might not be real. This piece of paper that I held in my hand, that I'd just taken from an envelope as I was opening my mail, was absolutely, definitely real. Not a folktale, not a myth, not a joke, not even a hallucination. Real. And a real threat. It said, in letters that had been cut from a magazine and pasted on the paper, just like on TV: Knock it off or you will be sorry!

Chapter Ten

I decided not to tell Len about the threatening letter. I still felt a little guilty, somehow, that I'd dragged him into all my concerns about people at the Hall when he was having those terrible problems of his own. Since it was Saturday we were going out—to the movies, taking Samantha with us. I was glad she'd be along, her presence would make it impossible for me to talk to him about threatening letters or ghosts or nasty rumors that make you lose patients. In the meantime, what should I do with this awful letter?

I was in the bathroom about to tear it into little pieces and flush it down the toilet, when I thought better of it. No, I should keep it just in case... In case something else, something more, something worse should happen. It was evidence—I knew that, I didn't watch TV for nothing.

I hated this. More and more I felt as if I were in a bad movie. I left the bathroom with the hated letter in my hand. Where to put it? I should hide it somewhere my daughter couldn't find it. That was ridiculous, even if she did find it she couldn't read it. She could only read words like ball and tall and wall....

My head was going round and round, I was making myself dizzy with, with...something. Anxiety, I supposed. I stood in my room and took a few deep breaths, breathing from the diaphragm. Cure for panic attacks, deep regular breathing, in and out. The out part was important—too much breath in and not enough out builds up carbon monoxide and causes hyperventilation. I was thinking like a nurse, and that was okay, that was real. After all, I was a nurse. But I felt unreal again when I hid the threatening letter in the best place I could think of: between the mattress and box spring of my bed.

Len and Samantha and I got through the movie and pizza afterward without a hitch. In fact, we had a good time. Not a single unsettling subject was discussed. I even managed to sleep well through the night, forgetting what I had hidden within my bed.

Then Sunday came and it most definitely was not a day of rest. The obscene phone calls began again. With a vengeance. He—it had to be someone male making that kind of awful panting sound, didn't it?— called four times.

"WHATCHA THINKING 'bout, Mommy?" asked Samantha at the dinner table.

"Nothing, honey. Eat your chicken. There's chocolate cake for dessert if you eat all your broccoli, too."

"I already did eat my chicken. You didn't notice, cause you're thinking bout something. I can tell."

I looked over at her and saw how solemnly she nodded her head. My wise child.

"You didn't eat your chicken, either," she pointed out.

Indeed I hadn't. I'd lost my appetite. Unconsciously I glanced at the wall telephone, and as I did I felt a tremor go through my body. I forced a smile, and then for her sake I lied to my daughter. "I was thinking about what fun we had last night."

"We sure did! I wisht Len was having supper with us tonight. Why didn't you ask him, Mommy? I bet he would've liked the way you cook chicken."

"I didn't ask him because I had other things to do today, and I expect he did, too. And because—"

The phone rang, and I froze. It rang again, and before I could move or think, Samantha had jumped up from the table saying in her childish treble, "I'll get it!"

I moved to stop her, and then choked back the cry, "No!" that rose in my throat. To alarm my daughter was absolutely the wrong thing to do.

"This is Samantha Matthews," she said, and then, "Oh, hi." She held out the receiver to me. "It's for you, Mommy. It's Frederick's mother."

Frederick was a boy in Samantha's class, the Four's. I let out my breath in a sigh of relief and took the phone. She wanted me to make cookies for a bake sale at the mall to raise money for the nursery school, and I agreed.

There were no more obscene calls on Sunday, but I knew now that the others I'd received weeks earlier had not come by accident. Someone had my unlisted number, and would call again. I'd just been lucky that Samantha had been playing outside all afternoon but eventually she was bound to answer one of the obscene calls. Unless I told her she couldn't answer the phone anymore, and that would make her unhappy because I'd praised her often for the grown-up way she handled the telephone. Answering the telephone was for her a privilege, one I couldn't take away without giving her an explanation.

I sat in the living room with a book open in my lap, but I wasn't reading. I couldn't keep my attention on the story, it was all just words on the page. I wondered if I should tell the police about the phone calls, and about the threatening letter. I wasn't really worried for myself, but I didn't want anyone to scare my daughter.

What I really didn't understand was why anyone should want to scare me. Maybe scare was too strong a word. More like annoy, harass. What had that letter said, exactly? Knock it off or you will be sorry. Knock what off? I hadn't done a single thing any differently in the last few weeks than I'd been doing all summer, so what was there to knock off?

I rested my head against the back of my chair and closed my eyes. Somewhere in the back of my mind I had a dim recollection of something I knew that would help me to figure this out, if I could just think what it was.... Not something recent, but a long time ago. Not here in Natchez. Before here.... On the base.

Of course! My eyes flew open as the memory came back to me all of a piece. We'd been living on the base, Sam Matthews and I, when a neighbor up the street had this same sort of a problem! She'd had a persistent obscene phone caller, and it had been scary because she'd even changed her phone number from listed to unlisted and the calls had continued.

I remembered her talking about it—the calls had gone on for a long time and they weren't just heavy breathing, the man had said awful things. She'd put her husband on and her husband had heard them, too. The police had finally caught the guy, I didn't remember the details of how they did it but I did remember how he'd gotten her unlisted phone number. She'd written it on a check when she was asked to, for identification. The obscene caller had been a clerk in the store and he'd had an obsession with her, and that was how he'd gotten her number.

I could get a new unlisted number and be sure I never gave it out except to people who absolutely had to have it—Cottonwood Hall, Sam's school, friends. Len.

But there had been that letter, too.

Suddenly I was too tired to think about this anymore. The whole thing just made me mad, and I didn't want to deal with it. I just wanted to live my life, for heaven's sake, and whoever the nut was who was bothering me, he could just damn well leave me alone! If what he wanted was a reaction out of me, well then he just wasn't going to get it. New telephone numbers were a lot of bother, and I wouldn't let my life be upset even to that extent. No siree!

I got up in a huff, determined to do something nice for myself before bed. A long, hot bath with my favorite bubbling bath oil, that would calm me down.

THE TELEPHONE RANG before breakfast. My nerves leapt in response, but I got hold of myself and answered. "Hello."

"Hi, Amanda, this is Sally."

"Hi, Sally." What a relief! I walked with the receiver on its long cord back to the counter and finished spooning coffee into the filter as I talked. "What can I do for you so early in the morning? You're not at the Hall already, are you?"

"No. In fact, that's why I'm calling. I, uh, I'm having some trouble with my car and I wondered if I could get a ride with you."

"Sure. Tell you what, I'll take Samantha to school and then I'll come by wherever you have to leave your car to be worked on, and pick you up. Where will you be?"

"I—I, well, I'm not taking my car. They're going to pick it up here. Later. So I'll just walk over to your house if you'll tell me what time."

"Lucky you, to have somebody who'll do that for you," I said, wondering how she managed it. "Well anyway, I think I'd rather take Sam to school first, and I'll come back for you. I'll just stop in the driveway and honk the horn. Okay?"

"Okay. If it's not too much trouble. I mean, I don't mind riding to her school with you. It's on the way and everything, isn't it?"

I had thought to spare my daughter Sally's company because for some reason Sam had taken quite a dislike for our next-door neighbor. Several times from the window I'd seen that Sam would talk happily with elderly Mrs. Pence, from whom Sally rented her room, but if Sally came out and joined them Sam would hang her head and soon be back inside. If Sally came out alone to talk to her, Sam would sidle away. With my new impatience I decided that my daughter was being foolish, so I said to Sally, "Yes, her school is on the way but it means you'll be leaving for work earlier than you're probably used to. If you're sure you don't mind—"

"I don't. Not a bit," she insisted in a rush. "So I'll just come on over, okay?"

"Half an hour," I said. "See you then."

And Samantha, when I told her, got the whiny tone I hated so much in her voice. "Do we have to, Mom-eee?"

"Yes," I said firmly, "and you be nice. If you ever decide what it is about Sally that makes you uncomfortable, you can tell me, and maybe it will make sense to me. But until then, you might try being a little nicer to her, Sam."

"Samantha." She glowered at me in an unnervingly adult way.

"Samantha. Sorry, sometimes I forget."

"That's all right, Mom."

Mom? That was a new one, but I decided not to comment. Mornings were never my best time of day anyhow, and I'd had enough excitement already.

Sally chattered in the car. Most of the time, she directed her chatter toward Samantha—only Sally kept calling her Sam and to my surprise didn't get corrected. In the face of all Sally's chatter my daughter maintained a glum, and not exactly polite, silence. So I told Sally myself that we were using Sam's whole name now because she was growing up and in school full-time.

"Oh, that's cool. So what's her whole name?"

For a minute I thought, Nitwit! What in the world else could it be if she's been called Sam? But I just said, "It's Samantha."

"Samantha, that's a really pretty name. Much better than what Sally stands for, my real name, I mean."

Samantha didn't take the bait. Sally chattered on. "Sally's a nickname for Sarah. My real name's Sarah, but not just Sarah, it's actually Sarah Mae. Just like that, Sarah Mae, it all goes together, and I hate it."

"You mean it's a double name?" I asked, not because I was really interested but to take up the slack. Samantha's silence was becoming so obvious it was embarrassing. Thank goodness we were near the school now.

"Yeah. I hate double names, they're so hicky sounding. You know, like Billie Joe and Jim Bob and all like that. It sounds so, so *country*—"

Ah ha, I thought. So that's what's going on, the country girl trying to forget her roots. In defense of roots, not to mention unpretentiousness, I said, "Lilibet has a double name. Her real name is Elizabeth Anne, and nobody could ever accuse Miss Lilibet of being hicky." I turned into the school's drive with relief.

"Yeah, but she's just called Lilibet. I'll bet she hates double names as much as I do. Oh, is this Sam's school, I mean Samantha's? What a nice, big playground you have, and what a neat building! I'd just love to walk you to the door and meet your teacher."

"I'm a big girl, I can go by myself," mumbled Samantha, and pushed her door open and got out of the back seat quick as a shot. For the first time in her entire life, she left me without saying goodbye.

I rolled down the window, feeling bereft. "Bye, Samantha!" I called after her.

Sam didn't respond until she was through the playground gate. Then she merely turned and waved. She wasn't smiling.

"MISS AMANDA, can I talk to you?" asked Ephraim Jones.

It was near the end of my shift and I sat in the cramped quarters of the nurse's station, writing my notes for the day. It was unusual for him to interrupt, and I would have been glad to give him my time in any case. I put down my pen and said, "Sure. You want to talk here, or go downstairs where it's more comfortable?" He looked around, shifting uneasily, so I added, "If you think we should talk in private, I'm sure we could use Dr. Percy's office. He isn't here today."

"Well, yes'm, I think to be private would be good."

"All right, let's go down."

Len's office was never locked. The few times I'd been in it I'd envied him all that space, which he so seldom was there to use. I stood back and gestured for Jones to precede me, then smiled at Sally who'd heard our footsteps and come to her own door directly across. I said to her, "A little private meeting," although I didn't feel I owed her any explanation. Then I closed the door.

"Let's sit down," I suggested, gesturing to two comfortable arm chairs that faced each other by the long front window.

Jones nodded his big head, waited for me to sit, and then sat himself.

"So, what did you want to talk to me about?"

"About that Tom, that autistic man in the new wing. I'm worried some about him. You seem to understand him, Miss Amanda, and I just wanted to tell somebody who understands."

My pulse quickened. "I've been worried about him, too. What have you observed, Ephraim?"

Jones looked around rapidly. He seemed to be checking the room, afraid someone might overhear what he had to say. "He's not right. I don't know how to explain exactly—"

I leaned forward, encouraging. "Just tell me in your own words. You're a good observer, tell me and I'll understand."

"He's gone down since you've been by to check on him a while ago. Looks bad. His face is the wrong color. He's been getting quiet, too, late of an afternoon these last few days. I always check on him last thing before I go home, so I've seen how he gets. Next day, he's himself again. Today, though—" Jones moved his head slowly, negatively, from side to side "—today he's worse. I'm worried."

"That's good enough for me." I stood up immediately. "Come on, I'm going to see Tom Parker right now."

Jones looked as if I'd lifted a burden from him. He bounded up, and together we covered the considerable distance between the front door and Tom's room in the new wing in record time. One look at the young man told me all I needed to know: he wasn't getting enough oxygen. Jones had said his color wasn't right, and he'd been absolutely correct—Tom Parker wasn't simply pale, he was ashen, his skin had a gray cast and his lips were turning blue.

"You've probably saved this man's life," I said. "Now go, quickly, and get the emergency oxygen. You know how to give it, with the mask?"

"Yes'm." He took off and was back so fast I hadn't had time to complete the taking of a pulse. I didn't need an accurate pulse rate, though, to know that Tom's vital functions were shutting down. The oxygen would help, and if I could reach Len he could get here in minutes. I should call him first. I stayed until I was sure that Tom was taking oxygen from the mask Jones held to his face with one hand, while with the other he regulated the pressure on the tank.

"Good," I approved. "I'm going to call Dr. Percy, and if I don't get right through to him I won't waste any time, I'm calling the ambulance myself!"

I did reach Len, said I had an emergency and interrupted him with a patient, and he came. There was some confusion with the evening shift staff arriving and everybody wanting to know all at once what had happened. Of course the residents got wind that something was going on. Len worked on Tom and I got the point across that I was staying because this was an emergency, and I shoved everybody out the door.

In the sudden quiet, Len looked up at me. I'd never seen him more serious. "Do you want me to call an ambulance?" I asked.

"No, but I'm glad you're here. I want to keep this as quiet as possible. Get a basin, a wastebasket, anything. I'm going to try to induce vomiting. It's a Thorazine overdose, I'm almost positive."

Overdose? How was that possible, when I'd given the medication myself? I didn't waste any time arguing, I grabbed the plastic wastebasket and helped Len.

We worked in silence. Len got a gagging reflex and I knew he was right, we might be able to do it. If we couldn't, Tom would have to go to hospital emergency for his stomach to be pumped.

It didn't take long, after all. These rooms in the new wing shared a bath between every two rooms, and I was able to clean up the mess quickly and quietly.

I returned to the bedside and looked down at Tom. He was awake, subdued, withdrawn, and his color was back to normal. I'd seen it a hundred times before, but every time the recuperative powers of the human body amazed me. "He's going to be all right," I said.

"Yes, but I want to check him over more thoroughly before I leave."

"I didn't overdose him, Len."

"I'm sure you didn't, but somebody did." Our eyes met. I saw that he believed me. He said, "The oxygen was quick thinking, it bought us time."

"The quick thinker was Ephraim Jones. I told you he was good. If it hadn't been for him—" I looked toward the room's closed door, realizing for the first time that I'd lost track of Jones in all the confusion.

He was gone. I looked at my watch; I should go, too. I would have to skip the usual briefing conference with the evening nurse. This emergency had used up all our overlapping time and if I didn't go now I'd be late for Samantha.

I looked at Len. "I'm sure you'll tell me sometime, the sooner the better, why you wanted to be so quiet about this, but for now I have to go. Sam will be waiting for me."

He nodded. "Soon. I'll call you soon. And don't worry, I'll take care of whatever briefing needs to be done here. Thanks, Amanda."

I FORGOT COMPLETELY that Sally didn't have her car and I'd been supposed to give her a ride home. After I got my daughter settled with a snack and Mr. Rogers, who came on before "Sesame Street," I walked across the backyard and knocked at the door that was Sally's separate entrance to the house. She didn't come, and I thought that was odd because I'd seen her car out front. She'd managed to get it without my help, which made me feel somewhat less guilty about forgetting her.

I'd already turned away when I heard the door open, so I turned back. Sally leaned against the doorframe, inside the screen. I began my apology immediately. "I'm sorry, there was an emergency I had to take care of and I—"

"You don't have to apologize to me, Amanda," said Sally. There was a cold note in her voice which I supposed came from having her feelings hurt, and an insolence about the way she lounged there without bothering to open the screen or ask me in. "I saw you leave the Hall without me, so I got a ride from Frances Stark. She was leaving, anyway."

"I, ah, I didn't know she left that early. I thought she was strictly eight to five."

"She was *kind* enough to give me a ride home," said Sally pointedly.

"I see you got your car fixed," I nodded in the direction of the street where it was parked. "That's good. Look, Sally, I really am sorry. I don't usually forget things, or people—"

She interrupted me, straightening up and giving me a look that was venomous even through the screen. "I just guess you've changed a lot since you got so interested in that Dr. Len Percy, and him in you. I saw how he came running this afternoon, and I'm pretty sure you called him. I don't expect when he's around that you'd be paying much attention to anybody else."

"Sally! It was a medical emergency!"

She tossed her head, the bleached blond hair flew. "Yeah, I bet. Well, like I said, you've changed. I thought I knew what you were like, and I didn't, so you and your stuck-up little girl can just count me out, that's all!" And she slammed the door in my face.

I was stunned.

Chapter Eleven

It was Thursday, Len's office day at Cottonwood Hall. At my lunch hour, 1:00 p.m., he showed up on the second floor of the main house where I spent most of my time.

"Free for lunch?" he asked.

"I am. Is this an invitation for us to eat together?" I was always so glad to see him these days that I felt silly.

"Yeah." He leaned closer to me and lowered his voice. "Can you think of anyplace around here we could talk and nobody would much notice?"

There was a long silence while I pondered, and then slowly shook my head. The biggest problem was that if we did something like go into his office and close the door, Sally would see us—and she'd already made it clear how she felt about me and Len. I didn't want to add any more fuel to that particular fire. I still smarted from her tongue-lashing, and she was still carrying a grudge.

Len rubbed his head thoughtfully and, of course, mussed up his hair. Finally he said, "Okay. We'll eat together in the dining room, and if it turns out we have some privacy fine, otherwise we'll just be sociable. See you there in a few minutes.''

As I served myself from the silver dishes on the buffet I wondered, not for the first time, if I would like to live this way all the time. Today the hot dish was cajun shrimp, and I passed it up for salad and rolls and iced tea. I didn't think I really would like this kind of thing every day. In fact, now that the newness had rubbed off, I increasingly felt that there was more of greed and less of elegance here. It made me uneasy, and I was getting worn-out with shaking off uneasiness these days. I took my plate to a corner table and began to eat. No sign of Len—I was alone in the dining room.

He showed up a minute later and I commented, as he sat down with me, ''One good thing about you working here—you make sure you get a good big meal at least one day a week!''

Len looked at his loaded plate, then at me, and winked. ''I'm still a growing boy, I need this!''

''Um-hmm. Since we're alone and there's no way to know how long this desirable state will last, why don't you go ahead with whatever's on your mind.''

''I read the charts in Stark's office. Last night.''

''How did you manage that? Never mind, how doesn't matter. Did you learn anything?''

''Yes and no. And maybe how does matter, Amanda. I couldn't think of any other way so I did what you'd suggested. I called Stark and told her that I no longer felt I could do my job as staff psychiatrist without full access to all previous records, in the light of the unexpected problems we'd been having with residents. She didn't make a peep, she just told me to show up before 5:00 p.m. and she'd give me my own key to her office and the files. And she did!"

"Amazing!"

"Yeah. I was in there until the wee small hours."

"My heart bleeds for you. So what do you mean, yes and no? The suspense is killing me."

"I mean—" His tone of voice changed from quietly enthusiastic to objective professional. I saw why— the male nursing assistant who was subbing for Jones had come into the dining room and walked over to the buffet. Ephraim Jones had missed work for the past two days. I presumed he was sick, but didn't know for sure because nobody had bothered to explain his absence. I hadn't wanted to ask Sally, who took all incoming calls.

Len was saying in his professional voice, "I think we might do a finger-stick on Elizabeth Anne Bowe. What do you think, Amanda?"

"I think it's a good idea. She might be anemic." I'd told Len earlier that I wanted him to see her because she'd seemed more frail than usual the past couple of days.

Len called to the man at the buffet, "Want to join us?"

He got a "No thank you, doctor," along with a smile, in return. For a while Len and I ate in silence.

Eventually I said, "You usually see your private patients in the early evenings, don't you?"

"You know I do. People work in the daytime, I have to make a buck when I can."

"Then you won't mind if I'm unavailable by telephone evenings until around nine o'clock."

Len raised one eyebrow in question, and I leaned over, lowering my voice. "I've decided to take the phone off the hook every night until after Samantha's asleep."

He knew I was getting those annoying calls every night now, I'd told him. So far Sam had picked up the telephone for only one of the "wrong numbers," and like the first time, she didn't seem to have thought anything of it. But I didn't want it to happen again, and this was the simplest solution I could think of.

"Is it getting to you?" Len asked.

"A little. I can handle it."

"Okay, if you say so."

I was still dying to know what Len had found in the records. "Do you mind if I call you later on tonight?"

"I won't be home. As soon as I'm done here today I'm driving to Jackson. To see an old friend."

It was my turn to raise eyebrows.

Len grinned. "A guy. Old college friend. He's a lawyer now, thinks he's a big deal." Len winked exaggeratedly. "He's got connections with all those political types in the state government. It's a pain in the you-know-where, but I like to keep up with him anyway."

I got the point. Len was on to something, and all I was doing was running around in circles, getting nowhere.

I FOUND LILIBET walking slowly, unsteadily, down the long central corridor of the new wing. I wondered if a cane would be an affront to her dignity—one of these days she was going to fall and break a hip. Those small bones of hers were bound to be brittle, at her age.

I caught up with her and took her arm casually. "There you are! I've been looking for you."

She peered up at me, her face lighting up. "Amanda! How nice. Are you going to walk with me?"

"For a little while. How about a hike upstairs to the nurse's station? Dr. Percy wants me to check your hematocrit. He thinks you may be a little anemic."

"Oh, dear. Well, if it's really necessary."

We reversed our direction. I fitted my steps to hers and kept hold of her arm. "Miss Lilibet, would you allow me to get you a cane?"

"Think I'm getting doddery, do you?" She wasn't insulted, she was amused. Her blue eyes twinkled, and she stroked the ever-present ropes of pearls at her breast. "It just so happens I have a cane already, but I forgot where I put it. I have Alzheimer's, you know. I lose things all the time, it's so annoying."

It was true that she did lose things, and sometimes I'd have to go back to her room with her in the mornings because she hadn't dressed quite properly. And, she could get mixed up about what day it was, or even whether it was morning or afternoon—but on the whole she was still pretty sharp.

"Let's stop in my room," she said, "maybe we can find that cane."

As soon as we were in her room, her manner changed. She closed the door herself, deliberately. "I don't need a cane, but it's as good an excuse as any. I've been wanting to tell you about that key. They've changed the place they keep it, I can't find it anymore."

"Key? Oh, you mean the key to the ground floor stairway."

She nodded.

I pointed out, "It hasn't been locked again, I've tried it from time to time." The episode, which had bothered me when it happened, had quickly faded into the background. "Don't worry about it, Miss Lilibet. It isn't important anymore."

"I think little Sally knows I've snooped in her office. That's where it was, and I think she moved it."

"Miss Lilibet, I doubt Sally or anyone else would care if you seemed to snoop. Now, I can understand that you may not want to use a cane, but I would feel better if you carried one with you on your walks. So let's look for it, all right?"

We located the cane, then went upstairs and got her finger stuck. She wasn't anemic, which might have been a relief if I'd been less concerned about her general health. Anemia would have been easy to fix. I said so, but she only shrugged and looked away.

Lilibet trailed along with me when I paid my late afternoon visits to the residents and gave medication to those for whom it was scheduled—which was virtually everyone. I didn't mind her company. Her comments were often valuable, and sometimes pretty funny. Not lately, though, I realized suddenly. It had been a long time since Lilibet had said something intentionally funny.

When I was done with rounds she followed me back to my cubbyhole where I did charting before leaving for the day. "I know you have things to do," she said tentatively. Then she turned around in a full circle, slowly, carefully, with the cane over her arm. She hadn't put it to the floor once.

I thought she was preparing to take her leave. I took down the first chart.

Lilibet said, "There's a storm coming. Come out on the porch with me, Amanda."

I can get task oriented at times, and this was one of them. "I can't, Lilibet. I have to write notes in all these charts before I go off duty."

"Please?" There was a plaintive note in her voice that I couldn't ignore.

"All right. But not for long, I really can't afford the time today." Reluctantly I accompanied her through the French doors and out onto the porch.

She was right, the air had the unnatural stillness that precedes a thunderstorm. Nothing moved in the landscape, not even the cottonwood trees.

"It's the time of year for hurricanes," said Miss Lilibet, accurately. She sighed, a great, heavy sigh for such a small person. Unconsciously she took her cane in hand and put it to the floor, leaning on it as she walked right up to the screen. "I used to like the storms so much, but this summer, somehow...I don't know... I suppose it's just that I'm getting old. Or maybe there's a hurricane brewing out there somewhere. Something's coming, I know it. I can feel it in my bones."

As fond as I was of Lilibet, I was even more anxious to get back to my charting. If I was lucky I might finish in time to pick up Samantha before the storm broke. I wasn't a person who believed in premonitions, and so I paid no attention to Lilibet's words. Instead I said, "If you don't mind very much, Miss Lilibet, I'm going to leave you here to watch the storm come. I'd like to try to get away on time today, so that I can pick up my daughter before the storm breaks."

"All right," she said absently, but then roused herself. "Wait, Amanda. There was something I wanted to tell you, a reason I wanted you to come out here with me."

One hand on the French door, I waited.

She frowned. "I can't remember what it was!" Her hands began to tremble, and the tremor transmitted itself down the cane. Seeing this my heart sank—were these the first signs of the extreme agitation of Alzheimer's? Perhaps she really did have the disease.

But then Lilibet brightened. "I wanted to thank you, my dear, for telling me the story about Amelia. You know, our ghost. I knew, you see, that she doesn't really mean any harm. She just watches over the house, that's why she roams at night."

"You're more than welcome, and I'm sure you're right. She doesn't mean any harm." No, the ghost—if that's what it was—had simply scared poor Belinda into a coma! But there was no sense getting Lilibet all worked up again.

Nevertheless, her frown had returned along with some of the tremor. "I don't think that was what I asked you to come out here for, but it will do, because I did want to thank you. You're a good girl, Amanda. I'm glad you're here."

High in their tops, the cottonwood trees murmured, a first sign of high wind on the way. Miss Lilibet turned back to her vigil. I took that as a sign that I could go.

IT WAS SUCH blissful relief to know that the telephone couldn't ring that I left it off the hook even after I'd put Sam to bed. Feeling completely relaxed for the first time in days, I took my after-dinner cup of decaf coffee into the living room, put my stocking feet up on the coffee table, and slid the local paper out of its waterproof wrapper.

Halfway down the front page was the heading, in big black letters: Man Found Dead Under-the-Hill. And a subhead: Killing Presumed Drug Related. I didn't read the finer print beneath. In my relaxed state I didn't feel like reading about violence. I browsed through the rest of the paper, spending the most time on the comics and the advice column. I even read my horoscope, which as usual didn't have anything useful to say—I didn't know why I bothered.

I folded the paper neatly with the front page out, laid it beside me on the couch, and stretched luxuriously. But then, as I was reaching for the TV's remote, those big black letters again caught my eye: Man Found Dead.... I picked up the paper again, intending to turn it over so that I wouldn't have those words staring up at me, but instead I felt compelled to read.

The man whose body was found this morning in an alleyway in the unrestored section of Natchez Under-the-Hill has been identified as Ephraim Jones. He had been shot twice, at close range. Time of death had not been established at press deadline. Police say that no shots had been reported heard in the area. No suspects have been arrested, but the murder is assumed to be drug related. Jones, a black man, was twenty-three years old and worked at a local rest home. His mother, who identified the body, declared that her son was a good boy who had no involvement with drugs. The Chief of Police says an investigation is in progress and he will release information as it becomes available.

My hands shook so much that the paper rattled. I thrust it aside, gulping as waves of nausea rose in my throat. Ephraim Jones, dead. Murdered! Oh, my God!

Chapter Twelve

I knew the police would come to Cottonwood Hall and ask questions about Jones. Either Frances Stark had anticipated what they would want, or they'd contacted her earlier, because by the time I got to work Friday morning the pharmacy log had been removed from the nurse's station. This log was where the night nurse, who presumably had more uninterrupted time than either myself or the evening nurse, would do the official drug tally each day. The police, of course, would pursue their drug-related theory concerning Jones's death. Anyone who worked in a place where drugs were dispensed might theoretically have access to those drugs.

I expected the police to interview me. After all, I had worked closely with Ephraim Jones for weeks and I felt I knew the man. I'd never in my life had any dealings with state or local police, but being in the military for as long as I had made me feel like a sort of kindred spirit. Anyway, their uniforms didn't intimidate me, since I'd been wearing one sort of uniform or another for most of my adult life. So when I knew they were in the building because I'd seen their black-and-white car come up the drive, I began to go over in my mind what I wanted to say to them about Jones. First off, I would try to impress on them that he was not the sort of person to have anything to do with drugs—he wouldn't take them, and he certainly wouldn't steal them!

While I waited for my turn—they'd talk to Frances first, of course—I continued to think about how my interview with the police might go. I went about my morning routine in a half-distracted state, but no one came to summon me to the office downstairs. I thought maybe they would want to come upstairs and see where the drugs were kept. I finished my duties in the old part of the Hall, and still I hadn't seen hide nor hair of the police. I opened the French doors, went out on the porch and looked for their car. It wasn't there. They'd come and gone without giving me a chance to say my piece. I didn't know what to think.

I still had routine morning duties in the new wing. There was no choice but to go ahead with them. However, as soon as I was able to take a break, I went to the office.

Sally was at her computer. The door to Frances's inner office was closed. I wasted no time. "Sally, I'd like to see Mrs. Stark."

She looked up at me in the guarded, slightly hostile way she'd taken toward me since our misunderstanding. "You can't. She's not here."

"Oh." I felt so frustrated that I couldn't find words. I turned away.

"She went downtown, to the police station," Sally volunteered. I turned back. Bright-eyed, her hostility momentarily forgotten, Sally said, "They were here about Jones, and she said she would rather talk to them at the police station. You know, so that the residents wouldn't be upset by uniforms and police cars and all that. I was dying to talk to them myself, but she told me she can handle everything. She doesn't want the rest of us involved. I was kind of disappointed. I guess you are, too. Isn't this exciting, Amanda?"

"In an awful sort of way, yes, I guess you could call it exciting. I, uh, I'm disappointed right along with you—I wanted to talk to them, too."

"I know what you mean!"

"I presume Mrs. Stark took the pharmacy log with her to the police station?"

"No, it's in her office. They looked at it before they left and she had me make copies. You want to take the log back upstairs, Amanda?"

"I might as well."

"Okay. I'll get it." She disappeared into Frances's office and was back immediately. "Here you go. Listen, do you think he did it? Stole drugs from us and was selling them on the street?"

"No, I definitely do not! Jones wouldn't do anything like that."

Sally tossed her head. "Well, I think he must have. I think you never can tell just by looking at people what they might do. What else would he be doing down there in that part of town?"

I'd been to the section of Natchez called Under-the-Hill only once. It's down by the docks, on the river, and for over a hundred years was as notorious in Mississippi as San Francisco once was in California—and for similar reasons. Lately the preservation people had become interested in the historical possibilities of the place, and were doing some selective restoration and upgrading. It was not a part of town that I really knew anything about. I said, "I thought that area had been cleaned up a lot."

"Only the waterfront. There's all sorts of stuff goes on in the back streets and alleys, which is where they found his body. My boyfriend says—" She broke off, her cheeks pinking, apparently embarrassed that she'd mentioned a boyfriend. I found her embarrassment surprising, and rather touching.

"What does he say?"

"I, uh, I'm not supposed to talk about what he says to me." Now her cheeks were crimson and she blurted out, "He's married, Amanda. Promise me, swear you won't tell I ever mentioned that I have a boyfriend!"

I took pity on her. I was a little shocked, but she looked and sounded more like the Sally I'd thought I knew. I was glad of that. "I promise. Don't worry, Sally. Of course you would have a boyfriend, as young and pretty as you are, and whoever he is, it's no business of mine. Or anyone else's. So just don't worry, I've already forgotten. And besides, you didn't say anything anyway." I clutched the logbook to my chest. "Don't forget to tell Frances that you returned the log to me. I'd better get back to work."

"Amanda—" she called after me.

"Yes?"

Sally dipped her head, and for a moment she looked as new and raw as she had when I'd first met her. But only for a moment—when she raised her head again her eyes were hard. She said, "I haven't forgotten how you snubbed me, but I always liked you. I wouldn't have gotten you the job here if I didn't."

This was a kind of olive branch and I recognized it as such. I could ignore the part about her getting me the job, which was a rather insulting overstatement. "I never meant to snub you, Sally." I smiled. "Still friends?"

"Oh sure, we're still friends," she said. But she looked as if she still were not convinced.

"Good," I said, and went on my way, wondering how long it would take for Sally to come around. I did care; there was something about her that both puzzled me and tugged at my heart.

SATURDAY NIGHT I got the baby-sitter to stay with Sam, and Len and I went to the Melrose Inn. Our first date was here, I thought as I stepped into the dining room and felt a warm, nostalgic pleasure. I hadn't really known him all that long, yet it seemed as if we'd been together for years, as if we were an old couple. The waiter seated us at a corner table, near a window. The sky outside was turning purple as night fell.

"This is my favorite time of day," I said appreciatively.

"Days are getting shorter," Len remarked. "Which reminds me—what are you doing over Labor Day weekend?"

"Next weekend? Nothing special. I haven't thought about it." I began to read the menu.

"We should go somewhere. You and Samantha and I."

It was a nice idea, but somehow it didn't appeal to me. There was simply too much happening here, and I had too many other things on my mind. Len and I hadn't talked since his return from Jackson. I said, "Maybe. Sam would like that, I'm sure."

We ordered and batted around ideas about where the three of us might go, but my heart wasn't in it. Finally, after the waiter had placed our salads in front of us, I said, "I don't think I want to leave Natchez right now. Look, Len, you must have heard what happened to Ephraim Jones. If I don't get to talk to somebody about it soon, I think I'm going to burst!"

Len looked around the large room. It was filled with diners, and twinkled with points of light from the candles enclosed in hurricane glasses on every table. "Okay, we're secluded enough in this corner. But keep your voice down—you know you can get carried away. I don't know who to trust in this town anymore."

"About Jones. I wanted to talk to the police, I was so sure they'd interview everybody who knew him, worked with him. I mean, how else can they find out who murdered him?" I shuddered. "Ugh! I hate to even say that word—*murder.*"

"What did you tell them?"

"Nothing. They came to the Hall and Frances Stark whisked them right out of there neat as you please. Sally said she didn't want them to upset the residents, and Frances would take care of everything herself. She gave them copies of the pharmacy log, that's all I know.''

"The log wouldn't show anything. Logs can be altered.''

"Well sure, but—''

"By the night nurse. Do you know her at all, Amanda?''

"Not really. Surely you don't think Jones and the night nurse had some sort of collaboration to steal drugs and she was covering it up?''

"I honestly don't know what I think. Yet.''

I put my mind to work and ate in silence for a while. Then I said, "Tom Parker.''

Len raised one eyebrow.

I explained, "I'd be willing to bet anything that Jones never had any illegal doings with drugs, in or out of the Hall, but the last time I had any conversation with him was when he told me he's been keeping an eye on Tom. And you said Tom was overdosed on Thorazine.''

"You think Jones did it?''

I shook my head vehemently and as I opened my mouth to speak Len warned, "Watch it!''

In obedient low tones I said, "Ephraim Jones probably saved Tom's life. If he hadn't come to get me when he did, if nobody had looked in on Tom until the evening nurse made her rounds, it might have been too late. We both know that.''

"Um-hmm. About Tom—you remember I told you I'd read the complete records in Stark's office.''

Now I remembered. Learning about the murder had put everything else right out of my head. "And you said yes and no, as to did you learn anything from them.''

''Um-hmm. On the one hand, I can't find any fault with the way Frances has handled admissions. She admitted people whose records showed that they were stable and needed only custodial care. The kind of mentally ill people who, if they come from the other end of the economic spectrum, end up either on the street or in halfway houses, unless they're lucky enough to have family who will take care of them.''

''And on the other hand?''

''On the other hand, as you and I both suspected, there's nothing in their histories to suggest that any of them might have these dramatic, life-threatening episodes like Belinda Stokes had. And Tom Parker.''

''And Magnus Everett.''

''I'm not so sure about Magnus.'' Len shook his head, and his hair flopped down over one eye. ''I still say, he was so old that his death may have been just a blessing.''

''What about the new patient, Callie?''

''I can't tell about her. As Stark said, she'd been at home with her mother for years. There isn't much information. Her medications had been prescribed by a GP, and his notes aren't the kind you and I would want and expect.''

I was getting worked up again; I reminded myself to keep my voice down. ''Magnus didn't simply go quietly in his sleep, damn it! In fact, he was virtually in a stupor. He never should have been that zonked on what you prescribed for him!''

''Um-hmm.''

Slowly, the light of truth dawned on me. I went absolutely still, I felt wide-eyed with disbelief. One nurse simply does not suspect another, and yet I knew such things happened. "Somebody overmedicated Magnus. And Tom."

"Tom, for sure. As I said, I don't know about Magnus."

"And you think it was one of the nurses. Or maybe a nursing assistant."

Len sighed, and hunched himself over the table, with his arms on either side of his plate. "It's not that simple. In fact, it's so complicated that I can't point my finger at anyone, but I'm sure now that something out of the ordinary is going on. So I've decided to do something about it. At least for Tom. I'm going to get him out of Cottonwood Hall. I really believe his life may be in danger."

The waiter came back. We'd long ago finished eating, and I hoped he hadn't been hovering without our realizing it. I declined dessert, and Len asked for the check.

We were in Len's car before I had a chance to ask, "How can you get Tom out of the Hall?"

"Tell you in a minute. Let's cruise Under-the-Hill, and then go back to my place for a while, if you have time."

"I do."

Len headed for downtown. Natchez is built on high bluffs above the Mississippi River, and Under-the-Hill is so called because it's right on the river, "under" the downtown. As he turned onto Main Street he returned to our previous subject. "Back to Tom. He does have family, a mother and father who decided they couldn't have him at home any longer. I'm going to contact them and tell them that in my opinion Cottonwood Hall is not the proper place for their son. I'll suggest he might do better elsewhere, and make a couple of recommendations."

"Frances won't like that."

"Yeah. She just might fire my booty, as she'd put it. But I don't care anymore. I want him away from there, where he'll be safe."

I was concerned for Len, but proud of him too.

He added, "If she does fire me, I just hope she doesn't do it before we can get to the bottom of this."

I didn't talk anymore. I was too busy working on the puzzle. If *I* didn't overdose Tom Parker, and Jones didn't, then who could have? I muttered, "Where would they get the Thorazine?"

"It doesn't have to have been Thorazine," said Len, startling me. I hadn't realized I'd spoken out loud. I looked over at him and he caught my eye. "It could have been another drug that enhanced the effect of the Thorazine."

"Oh." He was right. I hadn't thought of that. I sat in silence, mentally reviewing all the drugs I knew.

As if he could sense my mental processes, Len said, "I did some research, you know, psychopharmacology stuff. Any of the sedative drugs would have the enhancing effect. Without some sort of direct evidence—"

"You mean like catching whoever is doing it in the act?"

"Yeah. Or maybe, if I'd been more suspicious earlier and insisted on an autopsy on Belinda—"

"Or Magnus."

"God, you're stubborn about him! All right. Or Magnus. Anyway, if we'd had an autopsy and I'd asked the pathologist to screen for sedative drugs, maybe we would have found the drug responsible. That is, assuming that there's more than simple overdosing going on. Anyway, it's too late now for autopsies."

"Yes," I agreed solemnly. "And let's hope that there won't be any more deaths to give us another opportunity for autopsy results. We'll just have to find out what we need to know some other way."

"Yeah. I'm working on it, Amanda."

I glanced over at Len. In the half light of the car's interior the lines in his face were invisible, which made him look more boyish than ever, and I remembered how Frances Stark had told me that Len was wet behind the ears. I said, "You know, Frances Stark underestimates you."

"Curse of my life," said Len, flashing the ready grin, "being underestimated. I've never understood it, myself. Care to enlighten me?"

I considered carefully before I replied. "I think it's because you have such a friendly face. You look as if you're continually about to smile, as if you're too much of a good fellow to take things very seriously."

"Well, in a way that's true. I was the middle child, so early on I learned to take it easy, to get along pretty much no matter what. Anyhow, there are times when being underestimated isn't such a bad thing. For example, I know how Frances feels about me. It gives me a certain amount of protection—as long as she keeps on underestimating me she won't be likely to suspect that I'm digging into this mess as deeply as I am.''

I thought about this, and decided that he was right. I said, ''One person who isn't likely to underestimate you is me. I give you credit, Len. You've done more work and more thinking about what's going on at the Hall than I realized before tonight.''

''Mm-hmm. Well, here we are—Under-the-Hill.''

I fell silent, and directed my attention to looking out of the car window.

RIDING THE FEW STREETS Under-the-Hill didn't tell us much that the newspaper hadn't already mentioned, for example that the alley was dark and the old warehouses were deserted at night. On the way to his apartment, Len told me what he'd done in Jackson. He'd asked his old friend, the lawyer with the political connections, to find out whatever he could about the Cypress Group.

''There's just one more thing, Amanda. It was the final straw that made me decide to ask my buddy for help.'' He mussed his hair. ''God, I hate to tell you this because it's so damn borderline, and I don't have any proof.''

''Go on.''

''There were no transferring medication orders in any of the original records.''

I didn't get the significance of this right off the bat. I asked, ''So?''

"You've said yourself, more than once, that all the residents at the Hall are on the highest possible doses of their meds. And you're right. I don't make up the charts, Amanda, and you don't, either. They're put together in the office. What I think is that the Cypress Group may have a kind of malevolent corporate policy going here. I think they want to be good and sure that once they get hold of these people who can pay and pay, that none ever leaves."

"You think Frances Stark ups the medications at the time of admission."

"I think it's possible. The others, the ones we were discussing earlier—I haven't a clue why they get worse. Because of Tom Parker, I have an idea how—"

"Drug overdose."

"Yeah. But not why."

LEN WOULDN'T ALLOW any more talking about Cottonwood Hall and related matters once we got to his apartment. He put on CDs and pushed furniture out of the way, and we danced. Slow dancing, bodies close, moving in sensuous rhythms with the music. He was a good dancer, and I'd forgotten how much I loved to dance.

If he was purposely tantalizing me, then he succeeded. I really wanted him to lead me into his bedroom. But he didn't. He took me home precisely at the hour we'd told the baby-sitter, and all the way back in the car I wondered why he didn't make love to me. Next time, I vowed sleepily to myself with my head on his shoulder, next time if he didn't take the initiative,

I would. I'd never had to do that with my Sam, but maybe Len was shy....

I didn't have to take the sitter home, she had her own transportation. That was fortunate because as soon as my head hit the pillow I was gone.

When the telephone rang my heart stopped even though I was still more than half asleep. In the darkness I fumbled for it on the bedside table. It rang again before I got the receiver in hand. My sleep-strangled voice cracked as I said hello.

It sounded like something out of a nightmare, that moist, heavy panting and blowing. Too familiar. My wits still dulled by sleep, I didn't have enough sense to be afraid. I responded with my primary emotion, which was anger, and I didn't bother to be careful about my choice of words!

Right over the panting noise, which was now being augmented by an occasional grunt, I said loudly, "Listen you ugly idiot, whoever you are, the police know all about this, and so does the phone company. There's a device on this line that's probably picking you up right now, so go ahead. Grunt some more. I really love that. And call back as often as you want, you hear?"

To my deep satisfaction, I heard the tiny click that signifies the other party has hung up. By then my adrenaline was pumping so fast that I had to get up anyway, but it was worth it. I went to the kitchen, drank a glass of orange juice, and then went back to bed and slept like a baby.

Unfortunately, that was not the end of it. I was again awakened by the telephone near dawn. My room was already light. This time, before I even said hello, an eerie voice speaking in a muffled, scratchy whisper said, "You'll be sorry, *bitch!*" And broke the connection.

I WAS TEMPTED to call the police. That had been a threat, in words that reminded me of the anonymous letter I'd stashed between the mattress and box springs. I got out of bed and wrestled with the mattress until I had the letter in my hand. I looked at the telephone, reached for it—then drew my hand back.

I sighed. If I called them they'd come over, and Samantha might wake up and I'd have to think of a way to explain to her. I didn't want to do that, didn't want to frighten my little girl.

I looked at the clock: six-thirty. She'd sleep for another half-hour, at least. I put on my robe and went out to the kitchen, stuffing the letter into my pocket. I might yet call the police; I didn't know what to do.

I made coffee, then opened the front door to get the Sunday paper. I walked with shuffling steps, I felt a hundred years old. The heavy, sticky, humid air engulfed me before I could retrieve the paper and get back inside the house. This was all too, too much—I wanted to move to Alaska.

Well, I'd feel better once I'd had some coffee. That first cup of coffee will always cure whatever ails you. The coffee was still dripping into the pot when I returned to the kitchen, so I leaned against the counter and unwrapped the paper, and took a look at the first page. Then I forgot all about coffee.

Chapter Thirteen

The headline said: Murdered Man's Body Dumped Under-the-Hill. The article went on to say that the medical examiner had concluded from the condition of Ephraim Jones's body and a subsequent investigation of the place where the body was found, that the man had been shot and killed elsewhere, and his body dumped in the alley near the docks. It went on to describe the autopsy results. Cause of death, a thirty-eight caliber bullet lodged in the heart. A second bullet had torn though the left pulmonary lobe and exited the body, missing the spine. Stomach contents . . . I didn't want to know what Jones had eaten for his last meal on earth. I scanned and soon found what I did want to know—subsequent detailed drug analyses found no traces of drugs in the body, no needle marks, no hardened veins. The body itself revealed no evidence that Ephraim Jones had been a drug user.

"I could have told you that," I muttered. Now I wanted that coffee. I got up and poured myself a cup before reading the rest of the article.

There wasn't much more. The police had interviewed family, friends and associates of the dead man—"You missed one" I muttered again—who all reported that they had never known him to use drugs, not even marijuana. Unnamed sources reported that Jones was not known to deal drugs. Therefore the police no longer considered the killing to be drug related. They were continuing their investigation.

I couldn't handle this alone. I went over to the wall telephone and called Len. "I'm sorry to wake you up on a Sunday morning—" I began.

"Amanda? Is something wrong?"

"Not with me, no. But there's an article about Ephraim Jones in this morning's paper. Let me read it to you."

I read it to him and he listened without interruption. I said in conclusion, "What's bothering me is that I don't understand why whoever killed him would dump his body in that alley. It's so close to the river. If they wanted to get rid of the body, which presumably they did or they would have left it where they killed him, they could just as easily have dumped it in the river and the current would have carried it away. It might not have been found for days, or weeks, or maybe even not ever."

"I'm not particularly awake yet, but I can think of a reason," said Len. "They wanted the body found."

"Oh," I said. All my body functions seemed to come to a dead stop. When I spoke my voice sounded strange. "You mean, as a warning."

"Mmpf," said Len, which I took for agreement.

The anonymous letter in my pocket, which actually weighed nothing at all, suddenly felt like lead. I opened my mouth to tell Len about it, and Samantha walked into the room.

Her face was rosy from sleep, her hair a mass of auburn curls, and she said, "Morning, Mommy."

I smiled at her, noticing that my face felt stiff, as if it did not want to smile. I said into the phone, "Gotta go. Samantha's up, and I want to fix breakfast. See you soon."

MY MIND WORKED a mile a minute while I made breakfast. Finally all that work paid off: I thought of a way I could talk to the police without involving my daughter. I took her to Sunday School, as I did irregularly, and instead of going to the adult class myself, I went to the police station. I took the anonymous letter with me.

The police sergeant I saw was not very impressed. He didn't even take the note for fingerprints because he said by now I'd handled it too much; to make matters worse, I hadn't kept the envelope. He told me how many obscene callers they heard about every week, and I was surprised that there were so many strange people in Natchez doing that sort of thing. As far as the sergeant was concerned, "You'll be sorry, bitch," was not much of a threat.

I felt like an idiot, but I stood my ground. Sort of. I asked if he wasn't going to inquire whether I knew of any reason someone might harass and threaten me. He glared at me then, but he asked me. I told him I worked at Cottonwood Hall, where the murdered

Ephraim Jones had worked. He perked up a bit at that, asked if I thought there was a connection, and all I could say was that I didn't know, I couldn't think of any. I was screaming inside, *Yes! There must be, and you have to find it!* But those were words I couldn't bring myself to say. Then the sergeant asked if there was anything I wanted to tell him about Jones, and I said I couldn't add anything to what they already knew, at least according to the newspaper.

After that, I really did feel like an idiot. His facial expression said so clearly *Lady, you are wasting my time,* that I simply left. I was sorry I'd come.

CALLIE WAS definitely worse. Most of the time she had no idea where she was. In a continual state of lethargy she sat and stared at nothing, made no effort to dress herself or to keep herself neat—everything had to be done for her. She was so anorexic, she seemed to be getting thinner every day. More and more often she refused to go to the dining room for her meals, and all residents were expected to do that. We didn't have facilities for bringing people more than an occasional meal in their rooms.

The only person who didn't seem to frighten Callie except for me was Sally Creech, who visited Callie at odd times just as she did with all the residents. But Sally had her own work to do, and Callie needed more than an occasional visit from chatty Sally. Finally, in desperation, I went to Frances Stark.

Frances surprised me. For one thing, she didn't look too good herself. Her dark suit looked a little dusty, as if she'd worn the same one for too many days, and her white blouse, which usually would blind you, had a spot on the collar. There were new lines in her severe face and circles under her eyes. Her manner was subdued as she heard me out—and that, too, was unlike Frances.

"So what do you suggest, Amanda?"

"If it's not against policy, and if she can afford it, I think we should hire her a companion. Not a nurse, not even a licensed practical nurse, but an aide with enough training to help her wash and dress, get her meals, that kind of thing."

"Is the woman still hallucinating?"

"Yes, some, but not so violently and only at night. The main thing is, Frances, if I didn't get her up in the mornings and dress her she'd lie in bed all day. I really think she'd just let herself waste away to nothing."

"And die," said Frances grimly.

I nodded, not liking the look on her face or the sound of her voice.

She turned her swivel chair away from her desk and looked out of her window. Her back was to me. "No, I'm going to have to refuse."

"May I ask why?" My voice was icy from the distaste I felt at having to talk to the back of her head.

"You may ask. I don't have to tell you." Frances heaved a huge sigh, hunched her shoulders, and then swiveled herself back to face me. "But I'll tell you anyway."

"I appreciate that."

"Her estate is contolled by a lawyer. A man I do not like to deal with. He would have to approve the extra expense, and we are already, as I'm sure you know, very expensive. It may be that I did make a mistake, as you and your friend the doctor suggested. That I should not have admitted her in the first place. Yet she came with the kind of referral that I cannot turn down. Now, I'm not going to say any more about this. You're a good nurse, you'll just have to do the best you can.''

I thanked her and left, disappointed and disheartened. Frances Stark was a brick, a rock, hard and strict, and I would have said until today, totally fearless. Something was wrong with Frances.

As I climbed back upstairs I realized that I'd been behaving in a contradictory fashion where Frances was concerned. I'd agreed with Len that things were not all they should be at the Hall, and that Frances must be at least in part responsible. Yet I still relied on her, had faith that she was always there even if she kept in the background, faith that as long as the reins were in her hands somehow this whole team of horses wouldn't run away.

I looked down the hall at Callie's room, and at the empty room across that had been Magnus's. We still didn't have a replacement for him, so there was an empty bed at Cottonwood Hall. And soon there would be another: Len had succeeded in convincing Tom Parker's parents to move him to another facility.

Was that what was wrong with Frances Stark? Had someone higher up in the organization called her on the carpet for losing residents? And for having problems with others?

"Miss Amanda, Miss Amanda!" The voice was Peter's. I turned around and almost bumped into his round, protruding tummy. He said, "Can I talk to you again?"

"Sure. You want us to go into your room?"

He bobbed his head, yes, and shuffled along beside me. We went and sat by the window, as before, and he began. "I saw, I saw it again last night. The b-black thing."

The look on Peter's face reminded me of that fairy story about the creatures with eyes as big as saucers, eyes as big as plates, eyes as big as mill wheels. His eyes just kept getting bigger and bigger. He gave me goose bumps, but I hoped I appeared calm.

"Can you tell me about it?"

"Miss, Miss Lily—"

"Miss Lilibet?"

He bobbed his head, eyes popping, "Miss Lilibet, she told us. She came around and told us it's a g-g-ghost! It's the g-ghost of Cottonwood Hall!"

At that moment I could gladly have locked my friend Miss Lilibet in her room and thrown away the key.

But Peter, continuing to bob his head, went on to say, "She, she said we didn't need to be af-fraid of the ghost. It's a nice lady ghost that looks, looks after the hall."

"Well," I said, relenting in my annoyance some-what, "in that case we don't have anything to worry about, do we?"

"N-no. But I still don't like, don't like it. I don't like the sh-shad-shadows. Looks like a mon-mon-monster."

"There aren't any monsters here, Peter," I said with certainty. I wished I could say the same about ghosts!

"F-feathers. Black feathers. I'm allergic to feathers."

What was this about feathers? Black feathers? It sounded almost as if Peter were turning schizophrenic, talking word salad. Yet the two words "black feathers" had a familiar ring. "Tell me more about the black feathers, Peter."

"It's the g-ghost—has black feathers. They st-stick out. Make bad shad-shadows. I was, was brave. Last night. I st-stood in my door and looked r-right at the ghost. And I saw the feathers. I made it go away! I'll be all r-right now, long as it doesn't come in my, my room with the feathers."

"Because you're allergic."

He bobbed his head.

I patted his hand. "You really were brave, Peter. Congratulations. Where was this ghost when you saw it?"

"Come-coming out of Callie's room. She, she doesn't scream at it anymore. Guess she's get-getting used to it. B-but know what, Amanda?"

"What?"

"I like it, like it here and all, b-but I wish we didn't have a ghost. Even if it's a nice lady ghost. "

"I understand exactly how you feel, Peter. And I'm going to do something about it. There are ways to convince ghosts to leave and go somewhere else. I'm going to find out how, and I'm going to make that ghost go away. Black feathers and all!''

He beamed, his round cheeks glowing. Peter had a sweet side to him that I hadn't known before. I wanted to hug him, but instead I squeezed the hand I'd just patted. "Be patient, now, because it may take a while, but I promise you I really will do it!''

I PLACED A PLATE of pot roast and vegetables that I'd saved from dinner in front of Len, and went back to the counter to make him a fresh salad. I'd offered to feed him if he would come over after his last appointment. Breaking lettuce into a bowl I asked over my shoulder, "Has it ever occurred to you that almost all the time we spend together, one or both of us is eating?''

"Yeah. It's because we're such hard-working people." He tried to leer, and it came out more of a ridiculous-looking grin. "I guess we have a choice: eating or sleeping. Together, that is. I vote for—"

Grinning myself, I flicked him with the dish towel, then set the salad at the side of his plate. "Never mind. Eat.''

While he ate, I told him of my conversation with Peter and the entire story of Amelia Everhard, aka the ghost of Cottonwood Hall. Finishing up, I said, "I've got to get in there at night, Len. I don't think there really is a ghost.''

"Well, of course not," said Len, munching dessert cookies.

"I thought there might be, until Peter was so certain about the black feathers. That's such a strange thing to say, I'm sure he must really have seen it. It's just too bizarre for him to have made it up!''

''Yeah. I like the part about him being allergic to feathers. Adds a nice humorous touch.''

''You're not taking me seriously, are you?''

''Oh, I take *you* very seriously, Amanda. Ghosts with black feathers, I don't know.'' He waggled his hand, a gesture that meant maybe.

''Black feathers, black feathers,'' I muttered. And then a bell went off in my head. ''I know! Magnus said that, the day he went so totally demented, only I thought he was saying black riders. He saw it too, Len, he must have!''

''Black feathers, black riders . . . I don't know. You have to admit it sounds nuts, Amanda. But if you'll ply me with some of that excellent decaf you make, I'll try to be serious about it.''

I complied. Then I said, ''I've thought of something that might work, but I need your help.''

''I'm game. What do you want me to do?''

''Stay here overnight with Samantha. My regular sitter can't stay past midnight, and the night shift doesn't even start until then.''

Len looked grave. ''If I stay here with your daughter, which incidentally is no problem, what will you be up to?''

''I hope I'll be substituting for the night nurse. Sally makes up the nursing schedule, and while I don't know for certain, it's usually hard to get nurses for weekends in general and nights in particular. I thought I'd tell her something has come up and I need a little extra money, so I'd like her to fit me in on a Friday or Saturday night."

"And if she does?"

"I'll see what the real story is on this ghost with the feathers!"

"Mmm."

"It must be a person, a man or a woman, dressed up that way. And probably, most likely, that person is in some way connected with the unexpected things that have happened to our patients."

By the expression on his face, Len didn't like my idea. I rushed on to persuade him, "I know I might not see anything unusual in only one night, I might have to keep it up for a while. But when I do, I'll confront this so-called ghost and find out who it is!"

Len shook his head. "Uh-uh. If you really want to know what I think, it's that we have a case of some sort of mass hysteria going on where this ghost is concerned. All of it induced by poor Miss Lilibet. The Hall is a little spooky at night, Amanda. And the residents aren't in their right minds, any of them. All it takes is a suggestion and a few of the creaks and groans any old house makes, toss in a few shadows, and there you have your ghost with the feathers."

"I don't think they're hysterical. I believe them, I believe they've seen *something,* and I think it's a person!"

"Well, if it is a person, and you expose that person, then you could be in danger, Amanda. I don't want you to risk it. Why don't you just be patient. My lawyer friend will come up with some information soon. We'll go that route—work behind the scenes, play the way the big guys play. Forget ghosts and go after the real problem, which is corporate greed on the part of the Cypress Group.''

What Len said made sense. In fact, I had to admit it sounded a whole lot more sensible than my plan. But I was itching to *do* something!

I made a last-ditch effort. ''Okay, here's a compromise. I work one or more night shifts. At least I can run a double check on the night nurse's routine—if she's been fudging the drug tallys I might be able to pick that up. And if I see the ghost I'll follow it *very carefully*. Maybe I can find out who it is. If I do, I won't do any confrontation. I'll just tell you, and together we can decide how to handle it from there.''

Len smiled, and put his hands up in the air. ''I give up! I swear, you have more tenacity in your little finger than most people have in their entire bodies.'' He became serious again. ''I love that about you, Amanda.''

The look in his eyes turned me warm all the way down to my toes. ''Then you'll help? You'll stay here with Sam?''

''I will. But I warn you—I'll worry about you every single minute, so you'd better be careful!''

Len came around the table, pulled me to my feet and into his arms. His kisses told me how much he cared. He murmured into my hair, ''Some day, some day—'' I cherished that unfinished promise.

I RAN INTO A PROBLEM I hadn't expected—Sally would not cooperate. She refused to schedule me for any extra time, insisting that the schedule was full and it would be too difficult for her to change it. When I pleaded, saying that I really did need the extra money, she looked at me as if she knew I were lying. I could tell she didn't believe me.

In my frustration, I thought of going to Frances Stark. Surely the administrator could override a secretary. If I could persuade Frances that I had to have a couple of nights' duty... No, that didn't feel right. I decided against it. Except that I still had Len's agreement to stay with Sam, I was back at square one.

Later that night, after my daughter was in bed asleep, I sat in my living room trying to figure out another excuse to be in Cottonwood Hall at night. There was one way, but it was really, really risky. Len would never approve. Of course, I didn't have to tell him...

There was a strange sound in the room. A sound that didn't belong. A scratching, scraping noise. Quite horrible, now that it got my attention, and loud in the room's stillness. *Scrratch! Scra-a-ape!* over and over. It grated on my nerves, akin to fingernails down a blackboard.

I began to feel as if someone were standing behind me. My couch was freestanding, facing a fireplace. It was possible for an intruder to be standing behind me. Possible, but not likely. All the tiny hairs on my body were erect. *Scrratch! Scra-a-ape!* My hands turned damp, cold, clammy. I dreaded turning around, and yet I had to.

I did, and of course there was no one there. The simple act of movement—or maybe the courage it took to move—had broken the fearful spell. Now I realized that the scraping noise came from outside of one of the windows on either side of the fireplace.

"Must be an animal," I said aloud to myself, "probably a raccoon." I strode across the room, jerked up the blinds, flipped the window latch and raised the window, making as much noise as I could.

"Shoo! Scat! Get out of here!" I yelled, banging on the screen. I didn't look until I was good and sure I'd given whatever had made that noise enough time to run away. Because I didn't really think it was a raccoon. Or an animal.

The phone calls had stopped. Now this had started, and this was worse. Much worse. The person doing it had been standing right outside my window. He, she, or it knew more than my unlisted telephone number. He knew where I lived.

Chapter Fourteen

There is no time in the world better than 3:00 a.m. for fostering self-doubt. I was willing to bet that even The Donald doubts himself if he happens to be awake between three and four o'clock in the morning.

That's what happened to me. I went to bed absolutely certain that if the scratching at my window screen came again, just one more time, I would call the police. I went to bed sure that this harassment was related to the stuff at Cottonwood Hall—somebody thought I knew more than I did, or was afraid I would find out more than I already knew, and was trying to scare me off. The same for the note, which I was totally convinced must have been pasted together by that same person.

And to top it all off, I was positive that Jones had been killed, murdered, because he really did know something. Which made this harassment even more serious. Yes, I would call the police if anything more happened. Anything.

Then I woke up and couldn't go back to sleep. When I squinted at the bedside clock, those cheery little red numbers said 3:00. The night was so black and silent it was like being in a void. All by itself, my mind began to question those things I'd been so certain about when I went to bed. I had some pretty wild thoughts, such as, do possums climb window screens? Possums are big and light colored, they do climb trees, so why shouldn't that lightish blob I'd seen when I finally did look out the window have been just a possum?

I kept up in this vein until I'd managed to turn everything I'd thought the night before completely around. Within an hour I'd persuaded myself that the heat and humidity of summer in the Deep South had rotted my brain, and spending all day five days a week with people whose thought processes are abnormal had finished off my already brain-rotted ability to reason. Somehow this comforted me, and I went back to sleep.

Oddly enough, it was the 3:00 a.m. thoughts that stayed with me when I got up the next morning. Oh, in the bright light of day I didn't think my brain had rotted, but I no longer had such a strong conviction that my petty problems at home had any relationship to anything happening at the Hall. Certainly not to Jones's death; and furthermore, Len and I were both probably wrong about Jones's body being dumped in the alley as a warning to people like him and me. Surely we were not that important—to believe that we were was an example of grandiose thinking.

And that is why, when the noise at the window came again that night, and the next, I repeated my routine of pretending that I thought it was an animal. I didn't call the police. I shooed, and the thing went away. And when I continued to wake up at three I got up and drank orange juice and watched the Shoppers Twenty-four Hour Cable Network until Real Karat Gold Necklaces and Giant Cubic Zirconia Rings put me back to sleep. Anything, even the shopping network, is better than doubting oneself at three o'clock in the morning.

During those two days Len had something to report. His friend in Jackson sent him a list of other rest homes owned by the Cypress Group, and he said that the Cypress Group was in turn owned by a holding company. I'd heard of holding companies but I didn't really know what they were, so I asked Len. He said it was a corporation that exists only for the purpose of controlling investments in a number of companies at the same time. This meant that very big money was involved, and his friend would have to do more digging to find out who were the movers and shakers of the holding company.

I felt lost, and said so. Len did not feel so lost—he had a piece of paper with names of other Cypress Group rest homes, and he was making plans to contact their staff psychiatrists, his counterpart colleagues. His goal was to find out—deviously, of course—if the other rest homes had policies similar to those at Cottonwood Hall. Maybe, he said, if he was lucky he might find another psychiatrist who had some of the same concerns that he did. I wished him well. Not only that, I wished I could do as much. Self-doubt had paralyzed me.

I could count on Miss Lilibet to do something to stir me up again. When I was about at my lowest ebb one morning she came tottering up to me. She had her cane draped over her arm where it didn't do her a bit of good.

"It's a beautiful day outside, isn't it, my dear?" she asked me. She was dressed all in ivory lace that might once have been white. Her shoes and stockings matched, but the stockings drooped a bit around her thin ankles, a pathetic touch.

"I think so," I said, "but I expect it's hot. We won't get any cool weather for at least another month."

"October is good," she observed, and I gave her two points—one for knowing that this was September, and another for remembering that October comes next. She went on, "They have the Pilgrimage now in October, too. Used to be they only did that in March. When I was young—you know, Amanda, I believe when I was young I was quite pretty...."

I smiled at her and continued with what I was doing, counting out medications into little paper cups while with one ear I listened to her reminisce.

"...and Mama and Daddy used to bring me and my brother Marcellus—I had a brother, did you know that? He was younger than I am but I outlived him. When he was little we used to tease him by calling him Marcy. He had such beautiful golden curls. I had beautiful golden curls, too. Mama and Daddy used to bring us to the Pilgrimage here in Natchez and— Oh, I just loved it! I loved seeing everybody all dressed up in hoops and crinolines. Just like in *Gone With the Wind*—wasn't that the most marvelous movie? When

I joined the United Daughters of the Confederacy—how old was I? I don't remember. Well anyway, when I joined I got to wear a hoop skirt under my dress, it was pink dotted swiss with bows everywhere, because my name is Bowe, you see...."

I hated to interrupt her when she was in such a good mood, but it was necessary. "Excuse me, Miss Lilibet. You can come with me while I give out meds if you like, but I need to get on with it."

"Oh, of course you do, Amanda. I don't think I'll go with you this time, but I did want to ask you something. What was it? I forget, I forget so many things.... Oh! Yes, I wanted to ask you, since it's such a pretty day, if you and I might go for a walk later. A long walk. Outside, under the trees."

"I don't know, Lilibet. It really will be hot, and the ground's uneven—"

She tugged on my arm and said, "Psst!" until I bent down to hear her lowered voice. "I have something to tell you. Something important! And I want to be out of this house while I tell you, so say 'Yes.' Please!"

That got me. "All right. Yes. I'll look for you when I finish my rounds."

"That's good, we'll have fun." She turned away and went off on her own, saying "Marcellus and I used to have fun. Oh how he hated to be called Marcy, because it was a girl's name but he was just the cutest thing...." When she reached the stairs and started down them she was still chattering to no one in particular about her brother. Once again I wondered how much of it was true dementia, and how much was an act.

She was sharp enough to remember our appointment, and to wait for me in a place she knew I'd have
to pass when I finished in the new wing. She tottered
out of the library and intercepted me. "Shall we go
now?"

I still had a tray full of tiny, now empty, cups in my
hand. I said, "Yes, as soon as I find a place to stash
this thing." I left the tray in Len's office, and we went
out the front door and across the wide porch, down
the long flight of stairs. She used her cane and I held
her elbow—it was like having a bird's wing in my
hand.

We walked slowly across the oval of lawn. At its
edge Lilibet stopped, turned, and looked back at the
house. She raised one hand to shade her eyes against
the sun, which bore down on us without mercy.

My main concern was to get us both into the shade.
I took her elbow again.

"It's a nice enough house," she said, consenting to
be led under the trees. "I so seldom get to see it from
the outside, you know. Now these cottonwood trees,
I can't say the same for them."

"Beg pardon?" I asked, not understanding.

She flicked with her cane at a bit of fluff that had
fallen from the trees above—the ground was littered
with it. "My mama used to say that cottonwoods were
such trashy trees—that was a bit of a naughty word
back then, I suppose she shouldn't have said that. But
she meant because they make such a mess."

"I see your point. Now, Miss Lilibet, we can't stay
out here very long. It's too hot, and it's almost time
for your lunch." And, I was thinking, task oriented

again, while all you residents eat lunch I'll chart my observations from morning rounds.

"You're so conscientious, Amanda. I see that, you know. I see a lot more than I let on."

"I've been aware of that, Lilibet. "

"I like you so much better than any of the other nurses we've had, that's what makes this so hard. I admit I've put it off, but it's bothered me that I haven't told you."

"Told me what?"

She straightened up as tall as she could, taking a dignified pose with one hand on her cane and the other on the pearls over her breast. "I have a message for you from our ghost, Amanda. She said I should tell you that you will be in danger if you don't leave Cottonwood Hall!"

I was too astonished to respond. Overhead the trees rustled, murmuring their secrets, dropping down dappled light.

Lilibet said, "Our ghost—poor, dead Amelia—is very concerned about her home. Something is not right, you see. But she's just a ghost, she doesn't know what it is. And I'm only an old woman, I know only what I feel. You should listen to her, Amanda. I know you wouldn't listen to me. No, that's not right—you do listen to me, you're ever so patient. But I don't expect you to feel you should do what an old woman says, especially a half-witted one like me. A ghost now, a supernatural presence from beyond, that's different."

"You're not half-witted, Lilibet, and you're much more important to me than any supernatural presence," I said, my sympathy for her bringing back my voice. "I appreciate what you're telling me, but—"

She cocked her head to the side. "You know I get dotty. Maybe not quite as dotty as I like to let on, but some days are better than other days. Today just happens to be one of my better days. Now, which part don't you believe, the part about the ghost or the part about something not being right?"

I was in an agonizing position, wanting to tell her the truth and yet not say anything that would hurt her. Finally I said, "I believe all of it, but I can't leave the Hall. Ah—" My mind, for days paralyzed on these matters, had slammed back into full gear and was now working a mile a minute. "Ah, you could help me, if you want to."

This she loved. She immediately looked five years younger. "Oh, yes, I always love to help!"

"Then tell me how this ghost looks, and what her voice sounds like, and when and where you usually see her."

"She's always dressed in black, so sometimes you can't see what she's wearing because it's dark, you know. But her hands and face are very white." She thought for a few minutes, screwing up her little face in concentration. "I've seen her walk just before storms—I told you that before—but not very often. Usually it's at night. Always in the old part of the house, sometimes upstairs and sometimes down. Once or twice she's looked so solid it was like looking at a real person, but usually I just get a glimpse, and then she's gone. I don't know what her voice sounds like, she whispers. I'm not sure I actually hear her, it's more that she whispers in my head."

"Lilibet, this is going to sound like an odd question—does the ghost wear a dress that has feathers on it?"

"Now that you mention it, yes. Not all the time, just the couple of times when she looked like a real person, then yes, she had a kind of feather boa thing all wrapped around her neck."

"And when she told you about me, was she wearing the feathers?"

"Oh, no, my dear. I barely saw her at all that night. She just whispered her message inside my head."

"Thank you, Lilibet." I took her arm. "You've been an enormous help. We should go back in now, we don't want anyone to miss us."

"But I didn't do anything yet!" she protested, looking disappointed.

"Yes, you did." Slowly I led her back out from under the trees. "There's something else you can do, too."

"What's that?"

"You can not worry about me. I'm going to figure out what it is that's not right here, and I'll be just fine. And one more thing—the very best thing you could do for us all is to tell Amelia, since you're on speaking terms with her, that she doesn't need to watch over the Hall anymore. She can rest in peace now. She has friends who are watching for her."

THERE WAS AN ENVELOPE with no stamp on it in with the rest of my mail. My name and address were carefully printed in block letters, the way a child would print only a bit neater. My heart rate increased when I saw it, but I stuck it between two pieces of junk mail and put it aside. Samantha and I had just come home and I wasn't going to open it in front of her. Maybe it wasn't what I thought it was, anyway.

"Mommy, can I play with the hose in my wading pool? Please? After I have some milk and cookies?" She didn't wait for an answer, she bounded down the hall to the kitchen.

Where do they get the energy? I wondered. She was already into the refrigerator when I arrived. Seeing me, she handed out my mineral water along with her half gallon of milk. Great, she could already take care of me. I could handle that. "Thank you, sweetheart," I said.

"You're welcome." She brought the cookie jar to the table carefully, using both hands. I got two glasses for us, put them on the table and watched in a kind of parental fascination as, again with both small hands, she poured neatly from the heavy milk carton and filled her glass without spilling a drop. Then she took a paper napkin from the holder and put three cookies on it.

"Want some cookies, Mom?"

"No, thank you Samantha. When did you start calling me Mom? You did it the other day, too."

"I expect when I get grown up I'll call you Mom instead of Mommy. Mommy sounds kind of more babyish. So I'm practicing."

"Samantha, you are priceless!"

"Is that good?"

"That's wonderful, and you're wonderful."

She smiled, munched for a while, and then said, "In Sunday School I heard a story about a pearl of great price. That's not the same as priceless, is it?"

"No, priceless is even better."

She looked quizzically at me.

I explained, "It's better because priceless means that even if you had zillions and zillions of dollars, you still couldn't buy it. Anybody with enough money could buy a pearl. But there isn't enough money in the whole wide world to buy a Samantha!"

She understood. She said happily, "I love you, Mommy."

"I love you too, Samantha."

THAT NIGHT I called the police, because the person or thing that scratched at the window screens threatened my priceless Samantha.

She came, rubbing sleep from her eyes, into the living room saying, "Make it go away, Mommy!" And immediately I knew what she meant. I didn't even have to ask.

I hastened to her and put one arm around her, the other finger to my lips. "Shh," I whispered. "Let's see if we can catch it, instead. Be very, very quiet!"

I picked her up and carried her into the kitchen. I was barefoot, we didn't make a sound. As we passed Sam's open bedroom door I could hear the awful scratching. Sam whispered, "It's a big wild animal, trying to get in!"

I whispered back, "Don't worry, it can't get in. I'm going to call somebody to catch it. Now you sit right here at the table. I'm not going to turn the lights on because I don't want to scare it away. Okay?''

I called the police emergency number and reported an intruder trying to gain entry to the house. Then I sat in the kitchen and held my daughter on my lap until they came—I held her more to comfort me than her. She'd been too sound asleep to be frightened. Yet. I was afraid the police themselves would scare her.

To give them credit, they at least didn't come up to the house with their siren screaming. But if I could hear them drive up, then the intruder could, too. Sam looked up at me. ''They won't hurt the animal, will they, Mommy?'' Like me, she could hear a thrashing now in the bushes; I didn't know if that meant they'd caught someone or if it were just the police beating the bushes. Either way, it was time to tell my daughter the truth.

''Sam, I mean Samantha, I don't think it was an animal. I think it was a person. That's why I called the police.''

''You mean like a bergerler?''

''No…not that bad. I don't think the person meant to come inside. Some people just like to bother people from outside their windows, and it's against the law.''

At that point there was a knock on my back door. Sam hopped off my lap. I got up and turned on the light and let the police in. There were two, a man and a woman, both uniformed.

''Evening, ma'am. You reported a possible intruder?'' said the man.

"Yes, I did." I glanced at my daughter. She was wide-eyed, but more in awe than in fright.

"I'm Officer Horn and this is Officer Hershey."

"My name is Amanda Matthews, and this is my daughter Samantha."

"Is there anyone else in the house?" asked Officer Horn.

"No. I'm a widow. Did you, ah, find the intruder?"

"There's nobody out there, ma'am," he said, and from that point on everything went pretty much the way I'd thought it would in my most self-doubting 3:00 a.m. moments. Except for my daughter's enthusiastic corroboration, in which she again referred to the noises she'd heard as being from a wild animal.

They were about to leave, when suddenly I remembered something. "Wait!" I said, "there's something else. Samantha, honey, why don't you take Officer Hershey into your room and show her what window it was."

"I forgot all about this!" I said excitedly when she was safely out of earshot. Sorting through the mail I'd tossed onto the kitchen counter, I found the unstamped envelope. Remembering earlier humiliation, I picked it up at one corner, using only my fingernails, and presented it to the officer. "I haven't even opened it, but I know what it is. I had another one just like it a few weeks ago and I did go down to the police station and report it, but—"

"And what," asked Officer Horn, holding the envelope by the same corner I'd touched, "do you think this is?"

"It's an anonymous, threatening letter. That's why I asked my daughter to leave the room. I don't want her to know how serious this is. Your colleague down at the police station jumped all over me for handling the other one too much. He sure can't say that about this. Go on, you do the honors. Quick, before Samantha gets back."

Officer Horn held the envelope by its edges and slit it. Carefully he extracted a single sheet of white paper. I felt vindicated when I saw the cutout letters, same as before. He turned it so that I could read it: You have been warned!

He said, "You had another one of these?"

I nodded, and he asked me to get it for him. Along the way I slipped into Samantha's room and saw that she and Officer Hershey were getting along famously. Hershey smiled knowingly at me and said, "Take your time."

Horn wanted the whole story, and he took notes. Someone was taking me seriously on this, at last! However, I was disappointed when I asked him outright if he thought there was any connection between this harassment and the murder of Ephraim Jones. He said he didn't think so, that they now believed Jones had been killed in a neighborhood argument and they were continuing their investigation along those lines.

He also said that he and his partner hadn't seen anyone near my house, or running away from the house, when they'd arrived. More than that, Sally had come out of her back door while they were searching the bushes, and she hadn't seen anyone, either, or heard anything. He promised he'd have their patrol cars drive by every hour and keep an eye on my house. That was all they could do.

Then he summoned his partner and they left. His parting words were, "I don't expect you'll have any more trouble, Miz Matthews. This type of criminal, once they know the police have been called in, generally move on to bother somebody else."

Somehow that was cold comfort. But my intrepid daughter said, "Wow, that was neat! I want to be a policeman when I grow up!"

THE NEXT NIGHT, on the other side of town, someone was tearing Dr. Leonard Percy's office to pieces. He didn't find out until the next morning, and he didn't tell me until the next evening. If I hadn't been so sure that Sam would regale Len with her story of the night the police came to her house, and how she wanted to be a policeman when she grew up, I wouldn't have told him what had happened to me. It seemed so petty by comparison, and when I did tell him, I said so.

"It's the same thing, in a different form," said Len. "It's another kind of warning."

"We should tell the police, then, that there's a connection between us, and Jones, and Cottonwood Hall."

"N-no," said Len slowly.

"Why in the world not?"

"Because I'm playing the innocent victim for all it's worth, and so should you. We don't want anyone to know what we know—or what we suspect. This could be bigger than we ever imagined, Amanda, and more dangerous. I'm learning a lot from my counterparts at the other rest homes of the Cypress Group. My cover story is that I want to relocate, and I'm just checking out possibilities at these other places because I want to stay affiliated with a Cypress operation. It makes sense, and they talk to me.''

"What makes sense is the relocation part. We ought to give it up, Len. We ought to just pick up and go. Except—'' I thought about Miss Lilibet, and Callie, and Peter, and all the rest. I even thought about Frances Stark.

Len was getting to know me well. He read the truth in my eyes and said, "Except you don't want to leave everybody, Lilibet and the others.''

I nodded. "Especially Lilibet. I don't want anything to happen to her. If she should turn like Magnus—'' I shuddered at the thought.

He took my hands. "Let's stick it out another couple of weeks. Everything I've uncovered so far is borderline stuff. I'd consider a lot of it unethical but I'm not even sure most docs would, and for certain I haven't yet found anything illegal. It's there, it's got to be. I can feel it in my bones.''

I nodded again. I could feel it in my bones, too. Only I thought my "it" was a lot closer to home than Len's. Yet he was the one whose reputation, whose entire future as a psychiatrist, was on the line. I had virtually nothing to lose by comparison. Except maybe my life. . . .

Chapter Fifteen

I checked with Sally one last time about extra duty on the night shift. I was casual about it, but I'd been so intense before that I figured the believable thing to do was to give it another try. I didn't think she would have changed her mind, and she hadn't.

As I was about to leave the office she said, "I saw the police at your place the other night, Amanda. So you had a peeper, huh?"

I had never in my life wanted so much to wipe an expression off of someone's face. Her mouth was twisted somewhere between a smirk and a leer, and her eyes held the kind of infantile maliciousness I hadn't seen since elementary school. I refused to be taunted. "Maybe. Don't worry, I doubt that whoever it was will be back in our neighborhood. The police are keeping watch on the house."

My words did the wiping off trick—her expression changed. Now she looked like a scared girl, overwhelmed by the dangers of town versus country. "I didn't know that. My room's at the back of the house, I can't see the street from my windows, only the backyard and part of the side. Geez, I guess you must have been pretty scared, and Sam too."

"Not really. As soon as I realized it could be a person out there, instead of an animal, I just called the cops. Samantha thought it was all great fun. Now she wants to be a policeman when she grows up. Excuse me, Sally, I'd better get back to work."

"Wait a minute. How is Callie? When I went to see her yesterday afternoon she didn't look so good. How is she this morning?"

Sally was a bundle of contradictions. She puzzled me. In the space of about five minutes she had seemed first malicious, then scared, and now concerned. I realized I'd never understand this girl, and I'd about given up trying.

Nevertheless I appreciated her concern for the residents and the way she spent as much time with them as her duties would allow. So I was glad to stay and answer her question. "Callie's about the same as she was yesterday. She's deeply depressed, Sally. That's why she's so lethargic and sleeps so much."

"Yeah. She was asleep when I went into her room. I stayed for a while but she didn't wake up, so I just left. There wasn't much else I could do."

"Well, at least you tried. Listen, I really have to go."

THAT DAY, and the next, as I went about my duties I worked out the details of my risky plan for getting into the Hall at night. I thought it would work, but there were a couple of things about it that I didn't like. First, if I got caught I'd be in big trouble. Maybe as big as

Jones. I just wished I could know for sure why he'd been killed—not to mention who had killed him. The other thing I didn't like was that I'd have to deceive Len. I had to let him think that I'd been assigned some night duty. If he knew what I was really going to do he'd want to stop me, and he could easily do that just by refusing to stay with Samantha.

I decided that Saturday night would be the night. Before that I'd have to do some shopping, and the things I needed to buy would arouse my daughter's curiosity. I couldn't take her with me. On my lunch hour I called Frederick's mother and arranged for Samantha to play at his house after school.

Other than all my mental activity, it had been a quiet week so far for me. Not so for Len, who had to put his office back together and reconstruct records that had been destroyed. He was also using his less busy day-time hours to write a journal article that he hoped to get published. A publication could help him establish a career that seemed in shambles almost before it had started. I knew he was also working on his suspicions about the Cypress Group. He had documentation of all his phone calls to the other psychiatrists. Fortunately he kept these papers in the briefcase that he carried with him. The office vandals hadn't been able to destroy them.

I should have known that the lull following my summoning of the police was only the calm before the storm. The proverbial storm began on Friday morning, and after that it never let up.

On Friday, when Samantha and I went to get in the car to drive her to school and me to work, we found that all my tires were flat. The car looked like a big crippled beast, and I felt personally attacked.

Samantha didn't notice. She skipped to the car and pulled open the door, as she always did. I never locked it; in Natchez there had never seemed a need to. I stood in the driveway with my mouth hanging open.

"What's wrong, Mommy? Why are you looking like that?"

"I, ah—there's a problem, honey. The tires on the car are flat. You go on back in the house. I have to check and see what it will take to fix this. "

"Okay. Can I watch TV?"

"Sure, fine."

I hoped that whoever had done this had just let the air out, that I could call the gas station and get the tires inflated and be on my way. I inspected all four tires, and all I could tell was that they had collapsed into puddles of rubber. I had an emergency inflator thing in my trunk, but it would do only one tire. I felt first helpless, then angry. I was even angrier when I called my gas station and they said they'd have to send their tow truck, they couldn't fix the tires here even if all they needed was air.

Samantha didn't mind, this was another adventure to her, something different that gave her an opportunity to watch more cartoons in the morning. I was seething by the time the tow truck had come and gone, and I'd called a cab to take us where we had to go.

I was also late to work. As I finally climbed the steps to Cottonwood Hall, I realized that I might have asked Sally for a ride. But her car hadn't been out in front of her house, had it? She hadn't answered the phone

when I called in, either. Frances Stark had answered
it herself, and I'd been so focused on getting my
problems taken care of that I hadn't thought that the
telephone should have been answered by Sally.

I went into the office. A young woman I'd never
seen before was at Sally's desk. I said, "Hi. I'm
Amanda Matthews, the day nurse. I'm late because of
car trouble, Mrs. Stark knows about it. Where's
Sally?"

"If you mean the girl that usually works here, I
guess she took a vacation day. I'm a temp from the
agency."

"Oh. Well, please tell Mrs. Stark that I finally got
here. I'll go on and make up for lost time."

I was a whole hour late, and the night nurse hadn't
stayed. She should have—by leaving before I'd arrived she'd broken one of the unwritten rules of nursing. Nurses just don't leave their patients unattended,
not even if they're "residents." I was incensed. Here
were our poor residents wandering around, some of
them still in their nightclothes. They were allowed to
go to breakfast in their robes, but I'd bet some of them
hadn't eaten. Thank God everyone was present and
accounted for, with no major changes since yesterday.

About ten o'clock the man from the gas station
called and said vandals had been at my tires, probably with an ice pick. There were so many punctures
that it would take a man almost a whole day's work to
repair them all. It would be cheaper, and faster, for me
to buy a new set of tires. Otherwise he couldn't promise me the car until noon tomorrow. I told him to go

ahead and put the new tires on, I wanted to have the car when I got off from work at four.

After that, the day didn't get any better. I felt as if gremlins had taken over the world and put Murphy in charge of the laws. The nursing assistant who'd taken Jones's place was nowhere near as good as Jones had been, and I always had to check after him—today he'd made a lot of stupid little mistakes that I had to correct. For some reason the residents were more alert, and therefore more demanding. Even Callie roused out of her lethargy, and sat by her window and cried. That was progress of a pitiful sort, and I tried without much success to comfort her.

By the end of my shift I felt as if I'd been been running on a treadmill all day, sweating to keep up, getting nowhere. I had the foresight to call a cab early so that it was waiting when I was ready to leave, and I sank gratefully into the back seat. It was blissful, after a day like I'd had, to let someone else do the driving. I decided to put my life back on the right track by picking up Samantha on time. If I picked up my car first I'd be late, and I'd had enough of that for one day. I leaned up and told the cabdriver to take me to the nursery school rather than the gas station.

When we pulled up in front of the school he said he would wait, and I told him it wouldn't be long. Happy to be getting my life straight at last, I went through the gate and into the building. I was a little surprised that my daughter wasn't waiting out on the playground, as she usually was.

Sam's teacher stopped me just inside the door. The expression on her face alarmed me before she'd said a word.

"We had a little problem here today, Mrs. Matthews."

My stomach knotted. "With Samantha? She's all right, isn't she? Where is she?"

"She's fine, and she's playing in the classroom. Under the circumstances I thought it best to keep her inside until you arrived." The teacher, a gray-haired woman with a kind face, frowned slightly. "I do hope I did the right thing. It's a relief to see you here."

"Well, of course I'm here. What do you mean, did the right thing?" Now that I knew Sam was all right my stomach unknotted, but I still felt uneasy.

"Someone else came to pick up Samantha, about an hour ago. A rather pretty young woman. All the children were on the playground, as they usually are at this time in the afternoon, and she came right through the gate as if she knew exactly what she was doing. But I'd never seen her before, so I intercepted her. I'm not certain, but I think when your daughter saw this person she ran back into the building. I found Samantha in the classroom, at any rate, and thought it best that she stay there."

"I didn't send anyone to pick up my daughter." My heart pounded wildly.

"She, the young woman, said you did. She said you had car trouble, and I recalled that you'd been late this morning because of car trouble. Samantha told us about the flat tire."

Not tire, tires plural, I thought. But I didn't say anything, I waited for the rest of the story.

"So I thought perhaps I was making a mistake by refusing to let the young woman take your daughter, but we have very strict rules here. If anyone other than a parent is to take a child from the school for any reason, we must have a signed note from the parent saying so. I explained this, and she tried to argue with me but I flatly refused to let her take Samantha. I hope I did the right thing! I wouldn't have wanted to inconvenience you. But since you say you didn't send her—"

I'd heard enough. "You did absolutely right. Thank you!" I started to rush off to get my daughter, but checked myself. "I, ah, would you describe the young woman for me?"

"She was very young, certainly no older than her early twenties, which is why I thought she might have been a baby-sitter. And as I said she was pretty. Blond hair, on the skinny side but, you know, filled out. She was high-strung, and did not have a very cultured manner of speaking."

Sally Creech: the description fit her to a *T.* I thanked the teacher again and went to Samantha. She said, "Oh Mommy, I'm so glad you came to get me. Sally was here and I didn't want to go with her, so I ran in here. That was a long time ago. I guess she went away."

"Yes, honey, she's gone. I don't know why she was here but it didn't have anything to do with you. I will always, always be here for you. You don't ever have to worry about that." I wanted to hug Sam tighter than ever and never let her go, but I gave her the usual squeeze and then took her hand to lead her from the building. I mustn't let her know how frightened I was for her.

I gave the cabdriver a generous tip for waiting so long. Then I paid for four new tires with my credit card. As I signed the slip I had the sinking feeling I always got these days where money was concerned. I might as well get used to it—there were bound to be more unexpected expenses before I was through this.

I told Samantha we both deserved a treat and took her to Burger King, even though it was too early for dinner. While she ate french fries with as many little packages of catsup as they'd give her, I tried to drink a milk shake that my stomach was not the least bit interested in.

Some sort of fundamental change was taking place inside me, built upon the fact that Sally Creech had tried to kidnap my daughter. I felt myself hardening, closing out the places where fear lurked, and anger. What was left was cold resolve, and intellect that felt sharpened to knife-edge. I had had enough. These things must stop, and I would stop them. Len would help. If he didn't, I would do whatever I had to do alone.

My mind worked swiftly, cleanly, and precisely. I looked at my watch: 4:45. There was a pay phone inside the restaurant's door, in full view of the busy serving counter. I said to Samantha, "I have to make a phone call, honey. I'm going to use the telephone right there by the door—see?"

I pointed and she nodded with her mouth full, yes.

"I'll be right back." I called Len's office number and spoke to the answering service that he used because he couldn't afford a secretary. I lied without a qualm, which never in my whole life had I done before. I said this was an emergency, that I was Dr. Percy's patient and I had to talk to him immediately because I was about to commit suicide.

It worked, as I'd known it would. Len immediately came on the line, and I identified myself and told him—turning my back to the room, talking fast and low—that Sally had tried to kidnap Sam, and I had to get my daughter to safety as quickly as possible.

"Don't go home," he said swiftly. "Come here. I'm with a patient now, but we'll finish up and I'll cancel the rest of my appointments. Let me help you."

"All right, but we won't be there until six o'clock. I have to take her shopping. I have to get her clear away from here, Len. I want her to think we're going on vacation. As a surprise."

"I have a cousin in Gulfport who has kids around her age. Want to go there?"

"Yes!" I said, feeling a rush of gratitude. "See you at six." I hung up and went back to the table. Pasting a smile on my face that was as bright as I could make it, I said, "I have a nice surprise for you, sweetie. We're going on vacation for a few days. Len is coming with us."

My credit card got a workout in the next hour. I bought one outfit of casual clothes for myself, and three for my daughter; plus pajamas and slippers for her, and as an afterthought, a bathing suit. I let her choose the color of a nylon duffle bag, so she picked green, her current favorite color. We stopped in a drug store for toothbrushes and comic books.

Sam seemed to be having a wonderful time until we got back in the car and I headed for Len's office. She looked out of the window and recognized that we were not going home. "Where are we going, Mommy?"

"I told you, we're going to meet Len at his office."

"And then are we going home?"

"No, sweetheart, we're going to get right on the road. We'll stop at a restaurant for dinner along the way. It's going to be lots of fun."

"But Mommy, I can't go anywhere without Mr. Winkie!"

Oh, God! I'd forgotten Mr. Winkie. Mr. Winkie was a brown teddy bear whose plush body had held up well, considering four years of constant loving. Sam never went to sleep without him. Could I persuade her that she was a big girl now, and could do without her bear for a few days? I didn't think so. I didn't know what to do.

I said tentatively, "Mr. Winkie won't miss us."

My logical daughter said, "Of course he won't, he's just a stuffed bear. But *I* would miss *him!*"

I glanced over at her, saw the slight pout to her lower lip, and my heart ached. She was too young to understand any of this. Ever since she was born I'd done everything in my power to make her life stable, predictable, reliable. Because she had no father, I wanted her to know that she would always have me, that her universe was safe and warm and loving. The next few days would upset all that. Samantha would probably need her bear. I promised, "We'll get Mr. Winkie. I'm sorry I forgot him. But right now we have to meet Len."

Chapter Sixteen

Under other circumstances I would have enjoyed Gulfport. The beaches were wide and uncrowded, the sand clean and white, the waters of the Gulf of Mexico were a beautiful, almost tropical, blue. The town itself had a tropical look and feel very different from Natchez or any other place I'd been in Mississippi. But Cottonwood Hall pulled at me, as if it had woven a dark spell around me and I could not escape. I knew I had to go back, and this caused my first real argument with Len.

We were walking along the beach, barefoot, in and out of the warm water as the surf rolled up and back, up and back. Sam was back at the cousin's house, playing with the other kids. It was the first real chance Len and I had had to talk.

"You and Samantha stay here," said Len. "If you don't want to stay with my cousin and his family—though Lord knows why you wouldn't, there's plenty of room and Samantha loves having all the playmates her own age—you can get a nice motel room."

"Nuh-uh." I walked head down, stubborn.

Len stopped and took me by the shoulder so that I had to look up at him. Or else be pointedly rude. He said, "Amanda, you do realize that neither of us is going to be able to stay in Natchez for much longer?"

"Uh-huh." We had already agreed that there was a conspiracy going on at Cottonwood Hall, if not throughout the Cypress Group. Sally wouldn't have been acting on her own when she'd tried to kidnap Samantha.

"Let me handle this. I have enough information at this point to go to the state licensing board. Maybe not enough to get the Hall shut down, it's all so damn borderline, but enough to get them to do an investigation. I'll go back and set the ball in motion, and then I'll just pick up stakes and leave, too."

"No." I shook my head. My hair was down; the onshore breeze picked it up and flung it in my face. I started to walk again, into the breeze so that my hair streamed back. I said, "My first concern was getting Sam to a safe place. As nice as your cousin's family is, leaving her here with them will be the hardest thing I've ever done in my life. But I'm going to do it." I felt again inside the hard, cold resolve, felt my mental processes knife-sharp. "There is something completely malevolent going on at Cottonwood Hall, a mere investigation won't make it go away. You know that, and I know that. Either we work together to make it go away, or I'll do it alone. I mean that, Len. I'm dead serious. I intend to be there, back at work, on Monday morning."

Len sighed. He rubbed at his head, mussing his hair. "I see you are. Okay." He pointed to a nearby dune.

"Let's go sit up there, out of the wind. I have something to tell you. There hasn't been time before now."

We climbed the gentle rise to the dune, our feet slipping and sinking in the warm sand, and sat facing the water. I waited for Len to go on.

"My friend in Jackson called Friday. You know, the one who's been looking into the Cypress Group for me."

"And?"

"The main mover and shaker in this whole deal is Melville Morrissey. Know who he is?"

I nodded, slowly. It was like being given the key piece of a puzzle—everything started to come together. "He lives in Natchez, bought one of the oldest, largest homes a while back. I remember he ran for an elected office in the town government my first or second year, but he lost. He's too nouveau riche, people haven't accepted him. He's been trying to buy his way inside by doing a lot of preservation stuff. In fact, he put a lot of money into Under-the-Hill."

"Yeah, that's the guy. You know more about him than I do, I guess because you've lived in Natchez a lot longer. But get this, Amanda—the man's dangerous. Dangerous and powerful, so my friend says."

"Money talks," I said bitterly.

"Morrissey controls the Cypress Group through the holding company, and a lot of other things besides. He may even have mob connections."

My razor-sharp mind came up with another interesting fact. "Last year, when there was all the talk about licensing riverboat gambling, using the docks down at Under-the-Hill, Morrissey was all for it. Of course, a lot of perfectly upstanding citizens were, too, but if he's connected with organized crime—''

"The gambling thing fits. I tell you, the man's powerful, Amanda. I don't see how we can go up against somebody like that."

I brooded. "Jones's body was found down there. In Morrissey territory."

Len moved closer and put his arm around me. "I don't want them finding your body down there, Amanda. Or mine. Look at me, please." I looked. He said, "I love you."

A yearning, pleasurable ache began in the vicinity of my heart, driving out cold determination. "I love you, too." His lips were tender, and slightly salty. His tongue, delicate and hot, traced the curve of my mouth. The merest taste, the gentlest kiss I had ever known.

I let my head fall to his shoulder. He stroked my hair. Finally I said, "It doesn't have to come to that. We must be reasonable, Len."

"Hmm?"

"I don't think you and I are really in any more danger right now than we were last week, or the week before that or the week before that. Sally doesn't know that I know she tried to kidnap my daughter. I'm glad my instinct was to get Sam out of danger as fast as possible, so I didn't go to the police. For all we know, somebody like Melville Morrissey could have dirty cops working for him. If I'd gone to them and reported attempted kidnapping, it would have blown this whole thing out of the water prematurely."

"I'm not following you."

"Okay. Let's back up. If you go to the state board, what will you tell them?"

"That we have patients at Cottonwood Hall who are mentally ill and therefore may be inappropriate for a rest home. Also, that they're not receiving proper psychiatric care, as in a regimen of psychotherapy designed to help them return to the community, and that perhaps they're being maintained on improperly high doses of psychotropic medications. I'd find a way to make all that add up to a charge that the Cypress Group has a corporate policy designed to keep people sick, so that they will continue to pay, rather than make people well. They're doing the same thing in their other rest homes. I don't have real proof, my phone conversations would be hearsay, but as I said, enough so that they'd have to start an investigation."

"You'd have a lot stronger case, wouldn't you, if we could prove that the patients are being given unauthorized medications? And stronger yet if we could prove that those unauthorized medications caused Belinda Stokes to go into coma and die, and Magnus Everett, and Tom Parker, almost."

"Yeah, but—"

"You said yourself that Tom had either been given an overdose of his medication, or another drug that enhanced it. Has it occurred to you, Len, that maybe Ephraim Jones observed the person who did it—whether Jones realized what he was seeing, or not? That Jones may have been killed simply because he'd been observing Tom Parker closely for days, and fetched me soon enough to intervene?"

Len withdrew his arm from my shoulder, pulled back, and looked at me with respect. He didn't say a word about me raising my voice. "God, Amanda, no! And you're right, you're right about all of that."

"Which is why," I concluded triumphantly, "we have to go back to Cottonwood Hall!"

BLESS HIM, Len made leaving my daughter a lot easier. He hunkered down so that he was looking her straight in the eye and said, "Samantha, I want you to help me with something."

She returned his grave look. "Okay."

He smiled at her, reached out and tousled her hair. "I knew you would. What a great kid you are!"

Since they were having this eye-to-eye conversation completely on their own, I stood by watching fondly. Actually it was more than fondly—my heart was about to burst with love for them both.

She grinned back. "You're great, too, Len. I like you a whole lot! And I really like this place, the beach is cool!"

"I'm glad you like it. Now, what I want you to help me do is keep a secret. It's about your Mommy. And me."

Samantha looked at him, then up at me, and back at him. She said in a stage whisper, "She's right there! You can't keep a secret from her if she's right there. And besides, I don't keep secrets from my Mommy. Not never."

Len laughed. "I don't care if she hears, I didn't mean we have to keep it from her. I meant it's about her and me, and I'm going to tell you so it will be our secret, the three of us. But there's something I have to ask you first. Because you, Samantha Matthews, are the most important person in the world to your Mommy."

Sam nodded, grave again. My heart turned over at her simple acknowledgement. Yes, she knew how important she was to me.

Len took Sam's little hands in his big ones. "May I have your permission to ask your Mommy to marry me?"

Sam's eyes got very big. I felt mine get even bigger, and prick with tears.

"You know what that would mean, don't you? That you would be my little girl, too. So is it all right? May I ask her?"

"Yes," said Samantha. I collapsed onto my knees and put my arms around them. I cried for joy, and nearly strangled them both, I hugged them so hard.

Len looked at me over Sam's head. "I take it the fact that you haven't clobbered me means that you also think this is a good idea."

I gulped. "I think it's the best idea I've heard in a long, long time."

We untangled ourselves and Len said, again to Sam but making eye contact with me as he spoke, "Now here's what we're going to do. We have to keep this our secret for a while. About a week. Your mother and I have to go back to Natchez, Samantha, to finish up some business. You're going to stay here with my cousin and his family."

Samantha was so bursting with happiness that she couldn't stay quiet any longer. She almost shouted,

"And when you come back we'll be a family, too! You and me and Mommy! I'm going to have a Daddy, you're going to be my Daddy, Len! Isn't that right, Mommy, isn't it just the bestest thing that ever happened to us?"

"Best," I said automatically, always the Mommy whatever the circumstances. "And yes, sweetheart, it's the very best thing!"

"I HADN'T PLANNED to do it exactly that way," said Len later. "It just kind of happened. I thought it would make it easier for Samantha to be without you for a week. You know, if she could believe that good changes were coming then this abrupt change—going to stay in Gulfport—wouldn't be quite so disruptive for her."

We were in the car on our way back to Natchez, and Len was driving. I tried to relax, my head back on the headrest, but every mile we got closer, the more I felt the net of darkness pulling me in. The darkness of Cottonwood Hall was more palpable to me than the dark night outside the car windows. The glow of happiness I'd felt with Len and Samantha in my arms was not exactly fading, but being pushed inexorably into the background.

I reached for the glow, and responded to Len. "You're so sensitive to other people's feelings, it's one of the things I love about you. I'm sure it's what makes you a good psychiatrist."

"Mmf. I kind of wish you hadn't mentioned my chosen profession. To tell you the truth I'd have, uh, gotten closer to you before now—maybe even asked you to marry me before now—if my life wasn't such a mess. I don't have the slightest idea how I'm going to support you and Samantha. We could have a rough time of it for a while. A while? Hell, it could take years for me to dig out of this hole I'm in."

"We'll be okay. Have faith. I'll sell my house..."

"The real estate market isn't great right now, you know that. And I wouldn't want us living off your money."

"Will you stop being such a pessimist, not to mention a male chauvinist? *Mi casa, su casa*—my house is your house. Which reminds me, I do want to go home. I want it to look as if I've only been on a weekend trip, no big deal."

Len glanced at me. I caught his eye, and the downturning of his mouth in disapproval. Finally he said, "All right, on one condition—I stay there with you."

"What?" I pretended indignation. "You want us to live in sin before we're married?"

He made the quirky grin. "I'll sleep on the couch if you want."

"Like hell you will!" I said happily.

MY GLOW WAS BACK. The darkness of a thousand Cottonwood Halls could not drive it away, because Len loved me. And I loved him. And together, we were splendor.

Making love with Len was like being naked on an infinite carpet of velvet, luxuriously unfolding and unfolding and unfolding. There was no such thing as time, only unending sensual exploration. Every touch was new magic, on and on, until we merged and became one beautiful, beautiful creature that moved with ripples of passion, heaved in tidal surges of pure joy. Linked together we went to a perfect world where I had never been before, and all was light, and hope.

Chapter Seventeen

The gremlins had continued their work at Cotton-wood Hall over the weekend. Worst of all was whatever had happened to Miss Lilibet; whatever it was, her chart said only that she had become "extremely agitated," they'd had to put her on Haldol. Haldol is a heavy tranquilizer that's often used with Alzheimer's patients, and agitation is an expected progression of the disease. I knew my own ambilvalence about whether or not she really had Alzheimer's was common, friends and relatives almost always felt the same way.

But oh, it was terrible to see Miss Lilibet sitting on a chair in her room, her head lolling on her neck, her frail body slumped. She had forgotten her pearls when she dressed, and without them her chest looked sunken, emaciated. Her hair was matted where she'd slept on it and not brushed it since she got up. She was breathing through her mouth, and she drooled a little.

"Lilibet, you sweet, dear woman," I said softly as I brushed her hair. Hearing a voice, she looked up at me, with no recognition in her eyes.

I couldn't stand this. I always let myself get too close to certain patients. I knew it was a failing in me, but I'd never been able to help it. I had to call Len about Lilibet—maybe he would take her off the medication. I left a message with the answering service for him to call me at the Hall concerning a patient. Then I went to see Frances Stark.

Sally was back at her desk. She looked as if the gremlins had been getting to her, too, which gave me a good deal of satisfaction. She told me that Frances was on the telephone, so I would have to wait.

I couldn't resist needling her. I felt anger deep below the surface, well under my new, cold control. I said, with a perfectly brilliant mock smile, "I had the best time over the weekend. We went to the beach, and the weather was beautiful. I hope you had a good weekend, too."

Her eyes were sunken, as if she hadn't slept for days. "I didn't do anything special, it was okay. I wondered where you were."

"Well, now you know."

She rallied a bit. "There was a strange car in front of your house this morning. I didn't recognize it."

One of the perks that goes with living in a small town—everybody on the street notices who's parked in front of your house. "That's Len's car. Dr. Percy. He stayed overnight." Now I was taunting her, though I kept my voice friendly.

Her face hardened, as if she wanted to glare at me but her dulled eyes were not quite up to it. She settled for saying, "So now he's sleeping with you. Congratulations, you're welcome to him. He's such a nerd."

Fine, let her think that.

She looked down at the buttons on her telephone. "Mrs. Stark is off the line. You can go in now."

FRANCES KNEW VERY LITTLE about what had happened to Lilibet over the weekend. She said the evening shift nurse had called her on Saturday to report that Lilibet was extremely agitated and upsetting the other patients. So they'd started her on the Haldol that was prescribed for such situations. Simple as that.

When Len called me back he said he'd come out and examine Lilibet if I wanted him to, but he didn't see any point in it. I'd told him the dosage she was getting and Len said that it was in line with protocol and she would tolerate it better in a few days. Exactly what I'd expected him to say. I hung up knowing there was nothing I could do.

Toward lunchtime, Frances came tearing through the corridors, looking like a harridan. Sounding like one, too. It seemed Sally had gone home sick, and it was too late in the day to get anyone from the agency. Sally *had* looked sick, I thought, and went about my own business.

THE NEXT DAY, Lilibet was no better, Sally was still sick, Frances was still looking and sounding like a harridan. I was preoccupied, making my final preparations for unauthorized night duty at Cottonwood Hall.

I'd had to tell Len what I intended to do. He'd taken some persuading, but finally he'd come around— which was a measure of how desperate we'd both become. He insisted that he would drive me over and come back for me afterward. That way, if I weren't waiting for him, he'd know something had gone wrong. I'd agreed that if anything went wrong he would have to get the police. But I didn't think anything would go wrong.

All day as I worked I went over my plans in my head. After eating lunch I checked the door inside the powder room to be sure it was unlocked. It was. In the midst of my afternoon rounds, on my way to the new wing I slipped downstairs, quiet as a mouse, using a slim flash that fit easily in the palm of my hand—I'd bought it specially for this—and I checked to be sure that the clothes I'd hidden in the exercise room were still there. They were.

Nobody saw me slip back into the corridor. Everything was working perfectly. I felt optimistic when I left at the end of my shift and headed home. Sally's car was in front of her house. So she really must be sick; if I were more charitable, if it's possible to be charitable to someone who has recently tried to kidnap your only child, I would have looked in on her. Instead I was glad—as long as she was sick, she couldn't be doing mischief at the Hall.

Then disaster struck.

I answered the telephone in the kitchen, where I was fixing supper for myself and Len. I heard his voice over the phone: "Amanda, something terrible has happened. I'm at the Hall. Miss Lilibet is dead."

"NO," I INSISTED through my tears. I'd used up half a box of tissues, "I'm going through with it. Tonight, just as we planned. Miss Lilibet would want that. Maybe her spirit will be there, helping me. But Len, are you sure, really really sure, that she died a natural death?"

He had cradled me next to him on the couch, and he stroked my hair as if I were an animal in need of soothing. Which I guess I was. He said, "I've asked for an autopsy and it can't be denied. This wasn't an expected death but yes, I think it was natural. It looked like heart failure. She collapsed in the shower, and the staff handled it properly. They didn't touch the body, they just turned off the shower and called me. I saw her there, right where she fell. She was crumpled up in the shower stall. I'm sorry, Amanda, I know how much you cared for her. But it's over now, she's dead, and she's at peace."

I cried some more, and Len stroked my hair some more. He continued to try to comfort me. "It's probably better this way. You've seen the progression of Alzheimer's. Would you want Miss Lilibet to suffer like that?"

"It's neglect!" I declared furiously, unwilling to let go of my anger long enough to answer his reasonable question. "Pure sheer neglect on the part of the staff! They shouldn't have let somebody as out of it on Haldol as she was take a shower unattended. There's something else about being on Haldol...but I can't think what it is right now."

"Hush, darling. Remember there will be an autopsy. If there's anything else the pathologists will find it. As for neglect, you could be right about that. We'll put that charge in with the rest when we write up our case for the licensing board, if that makes you feel any better."

I sniffed. "Yes. It does. And I'm going tonight, if it's the last thing I do."

"You are the stubbornest woman I've ever known!"

"Try tenacious," I suggested, drying my eyes, "it sounds better."

WE DROVE UP to the Hall at nine o'clock. My cover story, in case I encountered anyone as I sneaked from the front door to the powder room, was that I'd left a book I was reading on a table in the library, and I'd come back for it. I dreaded the long wait from nine to after midnight, especially on the spooky ground floor in the dark, but it was the best way. If I did run into someone that excuse would hold up, and even if I had to use it I could probably linger in the library and still slip downstairs.

"Actually, it's good that you could drive me," I said as we proceeded at snail's pace up the long, long tree-lined driveway.

"Glad to be of service," said Len, peering to right and left. "The part I can't figure out is how I'm going to turn the car around without going on up to the house."

"There's a wide space between the trees farther on. I'll show you—it's where I was going to leave my car. You can pull in there and I'll get out, and then you can back onto the driveway headed home. Simple."

Len grinned at me. "Amanda, I'm scared to death for you and I swear you're looking forward to this!"

"I am. I want—" I paused to find exactly the right word, "revenge. Justice. Knowledge. I want to know what is really going on here! But to tell you the truth, Len, I'd feel a whole lot better if it wasn't supposed to rain tonight. Do you think we'll have a thunderstorm?"

He shrugged. Well, he would, he was another of those born and bred Mississippians. "I doubt it will amount to much."

A minute later I said, "Here. Here is where you pull in and I get out."

Len kissed me, a little longer and a little harder than a simple goodbye kiss. He said gruffly, "Be careful, and be back here at 4:00 a.m. I don't want anything to happen to you. Especially now. You understand?"

"I understand. I love you."

"I love you, too."

IT WAS A DARK and stormy night, I thought, trying to make light of it as I scurried along the edge of the driveway, keeping near the shelter of the trees. This wasn't funny—it *was* dark and stormy. Like most clichés, the time-honored Gothic phrase had earned cliché status because it worked, it was true. Dark and stormy equals scary in anybody's book.

The cottonwood trees began to talk to me. I tried not to listen, not to imagine that they whispered "Go back! Go back." I told them to shut up, and strangely enough they did. In ominous, utter silence I came to the edge of the cottonwoods. I hung back behind a tree trunk and surveyed the Hall.

Light spilled from the second floor windows through the porch screen and made a bright pool of the front lawn. The downstairs windows were dark. I felt for my key to the front door in my pocket, assured myself it was there, and hoped I wouldn't have to use it, that the door was not yet locked for the night. From now until I reached that stairway door inside the powder room, speed was crucial.

I took a deep breath and ran across the lawn. My sneakered feet made no sound as I bounded up the steps, across the porch. I flattened myself against the wall of the house near the door, to catch my breath and to listen. I didn't hear anything at all from inside the house, but the cottonwoods started up again. They moaned and sighed. I reached for the doorknob; it turned in my hand and the door opened.

My heart pounded as I stepped across the threshold, but it was okay. Nobody was around. I closed the front door with a tiny click. As soon as I'd made it past the stairway, I'd be safe. I reminded myself to walk at a normal pace. I was only supposed to be here to pick up a book I'd forgotten. I felt as if I were moving in slow motion: past the darkened doorways of Len's and Frances's offices, past the formal parlor, the library... and into the powder room. Gently, gently I closed its door behind me.

I took my slim flashlight from the pocket of my jeans with one hand while I opened the stairway door with the other. Then I stepped onto the top step, in that claustrophobic space between the walls, and pulled that door shut. My entire body remembered that I'd once been locked up in here. I would have felt a whole lot better about this if I'd been able to get the key. But I hadn't, so that was that.

At least this time I had a flashlight. I turned it on, grateful for the narrow, powerful beam. The batteries were new, it wouldn't burn out on me. I was going to be fine. The hardest part was over, the part where I was most likely to be caught.

Well, maybe not the hardest part, I admitted. Len could have appreciated this—the hardest part was purely psychological. The vast room beneath the house, which had been scary enough by day, was a thousand times worse at night. I tried not to think about the house looming over me, but that child's game, *Heavy, heavy hangs over thy head,* kept running through my mind. There was one thing I hadn't thought about when I laid my careful plans— How to occupy my mind during the hours of waiting.

Well, first I could go on and change my clothes. I'd be safer once I'd done that, anyway. My safety was in my disguise: tonight, I would be the ghost of Cottonwood Hall.

I'd bought the clothes at a thrift shop, and they were perfect. A long black dress of crepe, with a moderately full skirt and long sleeves—it looked like an old formal gown, maybe from the forties. There were picked threads around the neckline where the former owner had removed beading or lace or something. I was already wearing a black turtleneck T-shirt, and I put the dress on over that. I remembered Miss Lilibet's description—all in black, with white face and hands.

However, to avoid detection, I would cover my face and hands. I didn't want anyone to see me at all. The same thrift shop had provided me with a black mourning hat complete with heavy veil, the kind nobody wears anymore. In fact, when I'd seen that hat I'd felt sure that I was getting help from Out There Somewhere. And I had my own black kid gloves, so skin tight that once I'd worked them on it was like having a second skin. I dressed all but for the gloves.

Then I ventured out from the exercise room with my jeans rolled in a bundle under my arm. I would hide them out here amid all the junk where it was unlikely they'd be found for years. When I left the Hall tonight, I would still be dressed as the ghost. I'd warned Len about that.

With my heart thundering against my breastbone, I shone my light over humped and hulking shapes, irrationally frightened that as soon as they leapt into visibility they would turn into something I didn't want to see. So much of this stuff was boxes, boxes of every size and shape. I didn't want to open up a box and stick my jeans inside, you never could tell what might be in a closed-up box.

A very interesting idea occurred to me: if someone were bringing unauthorized drugs into Cottonwood Hall, what better place to hide them? Well, if that was so, someone else could look for them. Not me. I was doing my bit tonight. I found an overstuffed, over-dusty chair not too far away and held my breath while I stuffed the bundled jeans under its rotting cushion.

Then I waited. And waited. And waited. Got scared to death that I'd been locked in again, and waited some more. It started to rain hard, so hard I could hear it all the way down here. I sat at the bottom of the stairs and closed my eyes every time lightning flashed.

At last, it was time. I went quietly up the stairs. My disguise made me feel like a different person. I said a prayer that was half to and half for the spirit of Miss Lilibet. I asked her, as I had once before, to communicate with the real ghost of Cottonwood Hall, Amelia Everhard, and tell her to rest in peace. Tonight, I walked the Hall in her place. Tonight, I was the guardian.

At the top of the stairs I gulped with relief—I was not locked in. I thought, *Here we go!*

The only thing upon my person that wasn't black as night was my flashlight, and that I kept concealed in the palm of my hand. I had even died my navy blue sneakers black, and inked the rubber part with black magic marker. I did not want to get caught up in the essential spookiness, or craziness, of pretending to be a ghost. I simply wanted to see what happened here at night. It should be relatively simple. All I had to do was remain unseen, and I could accomplish that by blending with the shadows.

Rain poured down the windows in torrents, but there was no more thunder or lightning. I thought, to be sure I'd covered all the bases, that I should first check out the new wing. I didn't expect to find anything there, and there were fewer places to fade into the background, but I'd do it.

It was odd, a product of the kind of imagination I'd said I wouldn't use when I was doing this masquerade, but I felt as if Miss Lilibet walked by my side. I almost heard her talk to me; I had to restrain myself from answering her.

Like a shadow I flitted from room to room. All was well in the new wing, except that there were two empty rooms now, Tom's and Lilibet's. I stood invisible in the blackness of Tom's doorway and watched the night nursing assistant make rounds, as I'd just done. He looked into every room, but not the unoccupied ones. I doubted he'd have seen me if he had looked; and if he'd seen me, he would have thought I was the ghost.

When he was gone, I flitted out, down the long corridor, back to the main part of the house. The fabric of my gown made an appropriately eerie rustle. I remembered to hold up my long skirt in front as I climbed the stairs. I didn't want to turn on my flashlight and the stairway was almost totally dark. I had to be careful.

With my head at floor level I stopped a few steps from the top. A night-light burned dimly somewhere in the hallway, making the few pieces of furniture cast monstrous shadows on the walls. I hadn't expected the night-light—my ghost act would have to be persuasive. Well, someone else had done it successfully, I could, too. Unless the only ghost who walked through Cottonwood Hall at night was the real one...and I doubted that.

It was not as easy as I'd hoped it would be to find a place where I could blend in with the shadows. Damn that night-light! I didn't want to stand in the open doorway of a resident's room because I didn't want to frighten anyone who might wake up to see me and think I was the ghost. But Magnus's empty room was too far from the nurse's station, and I wanted to observe the night nurse.

I couldn't continue to stand on the stairs. I thought the nursing assistant had gone off in the direction of the kitchen, but there was no guarantee he'd stay there. Taking a deep breath and holding it, I climbed the remaining steps and glided in my ghost-walk to Magnus's room. From there, I could decide where to go next.

There was a seductiveness about masquerading as a ghost, a temptation to glide from room to room, to watch the residents as they slept, to glide down the very center of the hallway. For a few crazy minutes I felt as if I were being possessed by Amelia Everhard. She seemed near, hovering. Wind flung the drumming rain against the windows of the room in which I hid, in great slamming gusts. I remembered the horrible white face I'd seen on the porch—not long ago, but it seemed like years. I heard footsteps, real or imagined, and my spine turned to ice. My hands began to sweat inside the gloves.

A faint jangle of keys accompanied the footsteps. I leaned against the doorframe so that I could see down the hallway. The night nurse was coming toward me, and suddenly I was no longer so confident of my disguise. I needed every ounce of willpower I possessed to stay where I was, not to shrink back into the concealing darkness of Magnus's room.

The nurse stopped halfway up the hall, next to a chest that I'd thought was simply a part of the decor because it was locked. However, she had its key. She also had the medication tray with its little cups. The cups were apparently empty, because after opening the chest she set the tray down on the floor. She went down on one knee and began to take bottles out of the chest, bottles that I easily recognized, and one by one she filled the little cups.

This was not quite what I had expected, but it was what I'd come to see. The chest contained an unauthorized stash of psychotropic drugs, the same drugs we used every day, which was why I recognized the bottles. What she was doing was as plain as the nose on her face: she was administering an extra round of medication, an extra dose of the prescribed drugs. I stood there and watched her do it; watched her then leave the second floor and go down the stairs, I presumed on her way to do more of the same in the new wing.

As soon as I no longer heard her on the stairs, I glided from my hiding place and down to the cubbyhole of the nurse's station. I had to be sure she hadn't tapped an extra supply that was legitimate if unknown to me. She hadn't. As I'd thought, no one was scheduled to receive medication in the dead of night.

The night nurse had left the chest open while she went to the new wing. I surveyed its contents on my way back to my hiding place in Magnus's room. There was nothing unusual about the drugs, except for the quantities stored in this secret place.

The rest of my vigil, which I kept from the doorway of Magnus's room, was unfruitful. No other ghost came, no black feathers. The minutes crawled slowly by, the rain slacked. Nobody moaned, nobody cried out, nobody screamed. I missed Lilibet with an ache so deep that it physically hurt—a good deal of my preparation for this night had been in planning what I would do if I encountered her in her own nightly patrol of the Hall. Now that didn't matter anymore.

It was time to leave. The night nurse had long since returned and was ensconced in the cubbyhole. The nursing assistant had returned to some other part of the house. Now, to get away.

With skirts rustling, I descended the stairs; I no longer bothered with my gliding imitation of a ghost's walk. My eyes were so accustomed by now to the darkness and to seeing through the black veil that I was able to move quickly. I unbolted the front door and stepped out onto the porch—they would find it that way in the morning, but it couldn't be helped.

The cottonwoods greeted me with sighs of welcome as I ran across the lawn. The damp night air had a hint of freshness that I appreciated. Once within the safety of the trees, I removed the hat and veil and tucked them under my arm. I shone my flashlight briefly on the face of my watch. I wouldn't have to wait long for Len.

In fact, I didn't have to wait at all—he was already there, he'd come early. His eyes scanned me from head to foot as I slid into the passenger seat, but he didn't say a word. His face was grave. I caught the silence, as if it were a disease. Now, when it was all over, I fully realized what I'd done. I understood why Len stripped the black dress from my body with such distaste once we were in the safety of my house. I knew why he crushed me to him and kissed me savagely. I did not share his anger but I understood it, and I did share his relief. He made love to me before either of us spoke at all.

Chapter Eighteen

"I think I should go on to work, as usual," I said.

We'd talked a little, slept a little, and now were at the kitchen table drinking coffee. It was, actually, a beautiful morning—recalling the freshness in the air around 4:00 a.m., I'd turned off the air-conditioning and opened the windows and the back door. Threats of danger to either of us seemed impossible on such a morning, but I left the screen door locked just in case.

"No way," said Len, who was not as optimistic as I was.

I realized that a good deal of my upbeat feeling came from a delayed reaction—I had risked a lot with my masquerade, and I'd been rewarded. Why not risk a little more? I argued, "But there's one piece of this puzzle still missing."

Len quirked his eyebrow. His mouth remained in a disapproving line.

I put my hands on my hips in the stance much imitated by my daughter. "Honestly, Len, you know what I'm talking about! Yes, last night I discovered an illegitimate supply of drugs. But nothing in that chest can account for what happened to Belinda, or Magnus, or Tom. And I have my suspicions about Callie. As for poor Lilibet . . !"

He sighed. "Sit down, Amanda. Please. Okay, I agree with you that what's being done by the night nurse is an extra dosage of already prescribed medication. Sort of an insurance policy that the residents can't make any progress, that they'll stay completely dependent on Cottonwood Hall." He mussed his hair, rubbing his head thoughtfully. "In fact, that explains why, for instance, Doc Stewart had so much trouble regulating Belinda Stokes on her lithium. And why you've continually complained that people are zonked, and I checked their medication records and didn't find reason for them to be as zonked as you described. That's enough, damn it! We can go both to the licensing board and to the police with that, we don't need to do more."

"I don't think the police would touch this with a ten-foot pole, Len. Unless we find out more, somebody is going to get away with murder." I picked up my cup, saw that it was empty, and got up to make more coffee in the four-cup pot that had always been enough for me living alone. As I worked, I said, "That's why I think I need to be there as usual today. If I'm not, Frances will get suspicious. Not to mention that she'll go bananas if Sally's still sick, and we're both out."

"I don't give a hang whether Frances Stark goes bananas or not. You put yourself in a lot of danger last night, and it will be a long time before I'm comfortable with you out of my sight again! Not to mention out of my reach!''

He reached for me, and I hugged him and kissed his ear before sitting down at the table again. He pleaded, "If you won't stay out of trouble for me, then think about Samantha.''

"No fair. That's hitting below the belt," I said. But it had the desired effect. My sense of exhilaration and false security faded. "I guess you're right. I guess we'll never know what caused the hallucinations and sent those sclect few into comas. Or why them, and not the others. . . .'' I fell to musing.

The only sound in my kitchen was that of the coffee drip, drip, dripping through the filter into the pot. A mocking bird was making a lot of racket outside. And from outside, another sound. Len and I, together, turned our heads toward the back door.

Sally Creech stood outside the screen. She didn't greet us, she pulled at the door but it was latched. She had a paper bag in one hand. She demanded, "Open the door, Amanda," and stood back.

"How about, good morning, Amanda, may I please come in?" I asked in a falsely pleasant voice, as I got up to do what she'd asked.

Len's hand on my arm restrained me, and he whispered, "Look!"

I looked. In one hand Sally held a paper bag. And in the other, a gun. My heart seemed to stop beating.

"Open this door right now! I swear if you don't, if you make a move anywhere except to open this door, I'll shoot right through the screen!"

I glanced at Len. He nodded, and I opened the door for Sally. She stepped through, and I stepped back.

"You, Dr. Percy, you stand up and put your hands in the air! You too, Amanda, go back to the table and put your hands up, where I can see them!" Sally looked dreadful. Her skin was sickly pale, her eyes were dark-ringed and bloodshot, her hair was as lifeless as dead corn husks. She slurred all the *s*'s in her commands.

I knew immediately that she was high on something. The cold logicalness came back to me—my mind began to click as clean and hard as a computer, and I felt nothing at all. No fear, no compassion for this obviously addicted girl. She hadn't been sick; she'd been home, feeding her addiction. I wondered if being high slowed her reflexes, if carelessness with the gun would work for me and Len, or against us.

"I guess you can sit down, both of you, but put your hands on the table."

We sat, and Sally plopped down hard in the chair that was usually Samantha's. She dropped the paper sack on the table. "Where's the spoiled brat?"

Len replied for me, "Samantha is with some relatives of mine. Far away from here."

"So you know I tried to snatch her," Sally said to me. The glitter of madness was in her eyes.

I nodded.

She continued to stare at me. For a moment her expression changed and she looked as young and confused as she really was. "I liked you, Amanda. I wanted you to have the job at Cottonwood Hall, I thought you really needed the money. I never thought you'd turn out to be such a nosy troublemaker. And him—" she twitched the gun in Len's direction, "—they never thought he would catch on. Plus, he needs money even worse than you do."

"Money isn't everything," said Len. "Who's the 'they' with such a high opinion of me?"

"Mel, mostly," said Sally,"but he got it from Frances."

"Melville Morrissey and Frances Stark," I said.

"Yeah." Sally reached for the paper bag but she kept the gun on us. "It's too bad I didn't get the kid, because if I had, maybe this wouldn't be necessary."

"You don't have to shoot us, Sally," said Len in his best trust-inspiring voice. "We were planning to go away today, anyhow. Just let us go. We won't say a word to anyone."

"I'm not gonna shoot you." She dumped the bag on the table, and a pile of large, red capsules spilled out.

Len and I looked at the capsules, then at each other. My mind clicked along; I could see that his did, too. I said to Sally, "That's chloral hydrate."

"Right again. Boy, you're really sharp today, Amanda," she said sarcastically.

Chloral hydrate is an old drug, a sedative, seldom used anymore. It induces a feeling of well-being followed by sleep, much like alcohol. In large quantities it can cause first hallucinations, then a slowdown of all vital functions, stupor, coma and finally death. Used in combination with any of the drugs our patients were already taking, chloral hydrate would enhance the effects of those drugs in addition to creating its own characteristic effects.

I said, "You've been taking it yourself, haven't you, Sally? You didn't miss work because you were sick. But you *are* sick, you know that, don't you? How long have you been addicted to chloral hydrate?"

"I'm not addicted! It's a good enough high, if you haven't got anything else. And I sure got plenty of these."

"Where'd you get them?" I asked quickly. I wanted to keep her talking, and I also wanted answers. She seemed willing enough to provide them.

"From my boyfriend." She grinned wickedly. "Melville Morrissey."

Len was stunned. "Melville Morrissey is *your* boyfriend?"

"He's married," I said in a sympathetic-sounding voice, "so Sally has been keeping the relationship quiet. Isn't that right, Sally?"

"Yeah. But I don't care if you two know because you won't be around long enough to tell anybody. You're gonna become instant addicts, that's why I don't have to shoot you. You're gonna swallow enough of those things to commit suicide together. That's what it'll look like. And then I'll call Mel and tell him he won't have any problems anymore. He's gonna be real grateful to me!''

While she was gloating I shot Len a meaningful glance, and got the same in return. Len said, ''Melville Morrissey must have been quite a catch for someone as young as you.''

''You said it! I was only eighteen, I met him in a roadhouse and it was like he was instantly nuts about me. Go figure—I couldn't believe it myself at first. He got me this place to live, and showed me how to do my hair and how to dress and everything. Then he made Stark fire her secretary and hire me. I was supposed to keep an eye on her for him. Imagine that, me, keeping an eye on old Frances!''

''So you must know everything,'' said Len, affecting awe.

''You bet I do,'' Sally nodded emphatically. She got a tinge of color in her sallow cheeks.

''Tell us about it. Since we're going to swallow all those pills anyway, you might as well,'' I urged.

''Okay.'' Sally leaned back in her chair, but she was careful to keep the gun trained at us. ''Mel saw a way he could get more money out of those filthy rich residents. He's in cahoots with this lawyer who like controls their estates, know what I mean?''

Len and I both nodded. We didn't have to pretend rapt attention, we hung on her every word.

''And the ones that didn't have any relatives at all, like Belinda and Magnus and that new one, Callie, the lawyer wrote their wills to leave all their money to Cottonwood Hall.'' She took time out to glare at me.

"That way, Mel ends up getting it. I trusted you so much, Amanda, that I told you about the Cypress Group. I was wrong to do that, I got in trouble. Mel was real mad."

"I didn't tell on you, Sally."

"I know you didn't, but Stark figured it out and she told. But I've been real helpful to Mel, so he let it go. He could always get rid of Stark. She was getting to be a real pain."

"So she wasn't in on it?"

"Nah. Oh, she reported to Mel, she followed the rules of the Cypress Group and everything. But she doesn't even know about the extra meds at night. The nurse that works at night, we got a deal with her. We could've had a deal with you too, Amanda. I thought we would, you'd have made extra money for keeping quiet. But soon as you got started working there, you were making waves. Next thing we knew, you were fooling around with this dumb thickheaded doc. Mel trashed his office and his reputation, but the doc didn't have enough sense to know when to quit."

I endured the hard glare of Sally's drug-crazed eyes and tried to ignore the names she called my lover, my friend.

Len didn't let her faze him—he complimented her instead. "You were the one who was smart enough to get the chloral hydrate to certain residents. May I ask how you did it?"

Sally offered him a sick, twisted smile. "It was real simple. I gave them a treat when I paid my friendly visits. Juice, or a Coke or something. You can open up these big capsules," she nudged at the pile with the nose of her gun, "and just dump it right in."

"That's very clever," said Len. "A few minutes later, the hallucinations would start. Unless you gave a little bit too much, and then they'd just sleep. Too deeply. You even came to see Belinda in the hospital, as well as I remember. "

"Yeah. I was a real faithful visitor." The sickly smile widened and became malevolent. "I killed 'em, all right! Mel was real proud of me."

"W-what about Tom Parker?" I asked, shaken.

Sally's face darkened. "I just did him on my own. I thought he was kind of cute, but he wouldn't pay any attention to me. So I gave him some of the stuff, just to see what it would do to him. He'd eat anything sweet, so I made some brownies for him, filled full of the stuff. But it only made him crazier, didn't kill him."

"Jones knew something about that, didn't he?" I asked.

"Yeah, he was watching me like a hawk. It made me nervous, so I told Mel and he just offed old Ephraim Jones!" Sally giggled. "Imagine that, Sally Creech having a boyfriend so powerful he can get somebody killed, just like that! And he did it for me!"

Bile rose in my throat. With an effort, I swallowed it down, but it rose again immediately because Sally said, "Now I'm gonna return the favor. I'm gonna kill you two, for Mel. Okay, now, divide up that pile. Half for you, Amanda, and half for the doc."

My hands trembled as I did what she asked. I glanced quickly at Len, then back at Sally. "One last thing, Sally. You were there at the Hall at night, too, weren't you? You dressed up as the ghost of Cottonwood Hall and went into the patients' rooms."

"Residents," said Sally automatically—she was certainly well trained. "Yeah, I did that. Took some of them orange juice in the middle of the night, with chloral hydrate in it. That Callie, she's a hard case. I'm still not finished with her."

"And your outfit, your ghost outfit—does it have feathers?"

"How'd you know that?" Hard suspicion lit in her eyes. "Miss Lilibet caught me, but I know she didn't have a chance to tell you."

"Lilibet!" I gasped.

"Yeah, that nosy ugly old woman. I was over there Saturday, making up the day I'd missed, and I got the nurse to put her on that Haldol she takes. But she was still talking and talking and I was scared somebody might believe her. I guess the feathers were a mistake. I found this feather boa thing, see, and it was black and kind of fun so I added it to my ghost costume. I don't know how Miss Lilibet figured out I wasn't a real ghost, but she did. Anyhow, I told Mel, 'cause I tell him everything. He got a guy to off the old woman, but he was mad at me for dressing up like the ghost. He didn't know I was doing that. I thought it was a fun thing, but he didn't look at it that way."

Len looked hard at Sally. "I thought Miss Lilibet died a natural death. In the shower. There wasn't a mark on her."

"The guy Mel got went in as a substitute nursing assistant on the evening shift. He just put the old lady in the shower and turned it on real hot. Mel said it would kill her, and it did."

Again Len and I looked at each other. We didn't have to speak to know that we both understood. A lesser-known side effect of Haldol is that it makes people unusually susceptible to heat, and can cause cardiac arrest under those circumstances.

"I guess that's enough talking," said Sally. "Amanda, get two glasses of water. You'll need it to get this much stuff down, and I want to be sure it stays down!"

For a minute neither my mind nor my feet could obey, because I was so shocked about Miss Lilibet. Then Sally trained the gun on me and barked, "Move!" and I stood up. My mind snapped on and began its cold, swift calculations. I turned on the water at the sink, reached into the cabinet for the glasses—

—and right below the cabinet was the coffeemaker with its full pot of fresh, very hot coffee. I moved so fast I wasn't even aware of thinking. I burned my fingers as I wrenched the top off the carafe and flung the scalding coffee right in Sally's face.

The gun went off, but Len had it, and I had Sally. Without her weapon there was no fight in her. She went limp as a dishrag, and started to cry.

I VISITED Cottonwood Hall one last time. Len was at home with Samantha; he had his arm in a sling—the one shot Sally fired before he got the gun from her had gone through his upper arm and grazed the bone—and Sam took great delight in playing nurse for him.

I saw with my own eyes what Frances Stark had told me over the telephone: that the residents, without their illegal extra doses of medication, were all more alert and some were even getting better. The fate of the "rest homes" owned by the Cypress Group hung in the balance. Probably they would be closed down when the licensing board finished their investigation, but Frances had been exonerated.

Sally Creech and Melville Morrisey had been charged with murder; his lawyer friend and the night nurse, with conspiracy. Under questioning, Morrissey admitted he had arranged for my harassment, as well as Len's—his aim had been to make life so unpleasant for us that we would leave town. All four were denied bail, being judged flight risks. Len and I would have to come back to Natchez to testify when they came to trial, but until then we were going to live in Gulfport. After that, the world awaited us—maybe we'd move to Alaska, where there would be no heat and thunderstorms.

There was one thing that still bothered me, after I'd said my goodbyes and walked down the front steps, out onto the oval of the lawn. I turned and looked back at the Hall, looked up at the porch, at the screens stretched between the great pillars at second floor level. Was there a real ghost in this great house? I did not know, and would never know, whose face I had seen that first day. I did not know, and would never know, what mysterious voice had spoken to Miss Lilibet and told her to warn me that I was in danger. It was not possible to know all the answers. Some things were better left in the dark—in the darkness of Cottonwood Hall.

Take 4 bestselling love stories FREE

Plus get a FREE surprise gift!

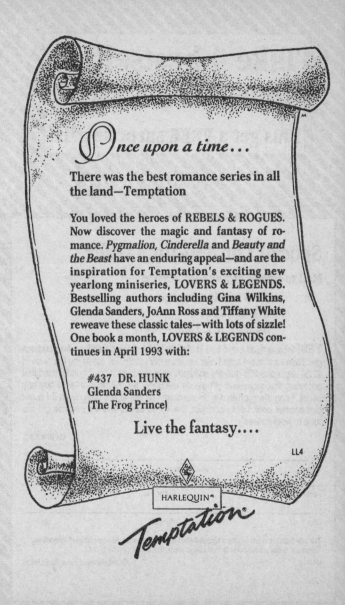

Once upon a time...

There was the best romance series in all the land—Temptation

You loved the heroes of REBELS & ROGUES. Now discover the magic and fantasy of romance. *Pygmalion, Cinderella* and *Beauty and the Beast* have an enduring appeal—and are the inspiration for Temptation's exciting new yearlong miniseries, LOVERS & LEGENDS. Bestselling authors including Gina Wilkins, Glenda Sanders, JoAnn Ross and Tiffany White reweave these classic tales—with lots of sizzle! One book a month, LOVERS & LEGENDS continues in April 1993 with:

#437 DR. HUNK
Glenda Sanders
(The Frog Prince)

Live the fantasy....

LL4

HARLEQUIN®
Temptation

Where do you find hot Texas nights, smooth Texas charm and dangerously sexy cowboys?

COWBOYS AND CABERNET

Raise a glass—Texas style!

Tyler McKinney is out to prove a Texas ranch is the perfect place for a vineyard. Vintner Ruth Holden thinks Tyler is too stubborn, too impatient, too…Texas. And far too difficult to resist!

CRYSTAL CREEK reverberates with the exciting rhythm of Texas. Each story features the rugged individuals who live and love in the Lone Star State. And each one ends with the same invitation…

Y'ALL COME BACK…REAL SOON!

Don't miss *COWBOYS AND CABERNET* by Margot Dalton. Available in April wherever Harlequin books are sold.